She's Back . . .

"When we get home, let's have a long talk," Nancy suggested. "I was too tired last night. There's so much to catch up on."

"That would be great!" Emily agreed happily. "I—I've missed talking to you so much."

She saw her mother smiling across the table at them.

Things are definitely looking up, Emily thought.

Breakfast lasted nearly two hours. The longest—and noisiest—family breakfast Emily could remember.

When they finally returned home, Nancy and Emily slipped off to the den. The shades were drawn. The room was dark.

Rich must have been up late, watching horror movies again, Emily thought. He always liked to pull the shades and make the room into a cave.

Emily fumbled for the light switch.

But before she could reach it, she felt Nancy's hands slide around her throat.

Emily uttered a choked gasp—as Nancy began to strangle her.

Books by R. L. Stine

Available from ARCHWAY Paperbacks

FEAR STREET®
R.L. STINE

The Stepsister 2

A Parachute Press Book

AN ARCHWAY PAPERBACK
Published by POCKET BOOKS
New York London Toronto Sydney Tokyo Singapore

AN ARCHWAY PAPERBACK *Original*

An Archway Paperback published by
POCKET BOOKS, a division of Simon & Schuster Inc.
1230 Avenue of the Americas, New York, NY 10020

ISBN: 0-671-89426-9

First Archway Paperback printing November 1995

10 9 8 7 6 5 4 3 2 1

FEAR STREET is a registered trademark of
Parachute Press, Inc.

AN ARCHWAY PAPERBACK and colophon are
registered trademarks of Simon & Schuster Inc.

Cover art by Bill Schmidt

Printed in the U.S.A.

IL 7+

The Stepsister 2

chapter
1

Nancy is coming home.

The words gave Emily Casey a chill. No matter how many times she repeated them in her mind, the words still excited her, upset her—frightened her.

I'm frightened of Nancy, she realized, hugging herself as she stared out through her bedroom window. I'm frightened of my own sister.

But I also can't *wait* to see her.

Emily stared out at the bare trees in her front yard, dark beneath a thin covering of snow. The bright late-morning sunlight shimmered off the snowy ground. Cold sunlight.

A white station wagon rolled past slowly, loaded with kids. The car skidded as it stopped at the corner.

Has it really been a year since I've seen my sister? Emily thought, chilled despite the warmth of the sunlight through the windowpane. Chilled despite the hot shower she had taken moments before.

She tried to imagine what Nancy's year had been like. A year in a mental hospital. A year away from her home, away from her family. A year of doctors and tests and . . .

Emily couldn't imagine it.

She was having enough trouble sorting out her own feelings. Nancy had tried to kill her, after all. A year ago Emily's own sister had tried to kill her.

Emily turned away from the window. She glanced at the clock. Time to get dressed. Nancy would be home soon. Emily's mother and stepfather had driven upstate to check Nancy out of the hospital and bring her back to Shadyside.

So much pain, so much unhappiness, Emily thought with a sigh.

It had all started after Emily's father had died in a boating accident. Emily had no idea that Nancy blamed her for the accident. Their mother married Hugh Wallner soon after. And Nancy and Emily gained a stepsister her age and a stepbrother—Jessie and Rich Wallner.

One big happy family. Except that fourteen-year-old Rich acted sullen and strange. And Emily thought Jessie was treacherous and evil. And Nancy . . . Nancy . . . Nancy . . . Emily's own sister, her older sister, the person she looked up to more than anyone . . . Nancy had tried to kill her.

One big happy family.

So much had changed in a year. Since Nancy was sent away, Rich had become more sullen, more closed-off than ever. But Emily realized she had been wrong—very wrong—about Jessie. Now the two were close, as close as real sisters.

And what will my *real* sister be like? Emily wondered. What will Nancy be like after a whole year away?

Will she be totally different? Will she still *hate* me?

Will she remember what she tried to do?

"I'm back," a voice called from the doorway.

Emily spun around with a gasp. "Jessie—!" She watched Jessie tug a carton into the room.

"I can't believe I'm moving back in with you," Jessie groaned. "After having my own room for a whole year."

"I can't believe you have so much stuff!" Emily exclaimed.

Since early that morning, Jessie had been moving her stuff from Nancy's room. "Save me half a dresser drawer—okay?"

Actually, Emily was glad to have Jessie move back in with her. It made her feel safer somehow.

Safe from my own sister, she thought wistfully.

Emily pulled off the bath towel she had wrapped around her wet hair after her shower. She shook her hair out, the way the models did on TV.

Only when *they* did it, their long, silky hair bounced magically into place. Emily's thick mass of curly brown hair fell in wet tangles. "Oh, great," she murmured, frowning into the mirror.

She didn't *hate* the way she looked. She just wished

she could do something about her wild and crazy hair. And she wished she weren't so big. "Big-boned," as her mother described her.

She always felt like such a cow next to pretty, petite, perfect Jessie.

Jessie had crimped, straw-blond hair framing her pretty, heart-shaped face, big, sparkly blue eyes, a beautiful high forehead, and creamy white skin. She reminded Emily of an angel she had seen in an old painting.

Emily brushed her hair, pulled it back, and tied it with a hair scrunchy. "I've got to get dressed. Nancy will be here any minute."

She glanced at Jessie, who was trying to stuff a stack of fashion magazines into the bottom of the bookshelves. Jessie wore a ratty gray sweatshirt and baggy, gray sweatpants. It doesn't matter, Emily thought. Jessie would look beautiful in a plastic garbage bag!

Giving her hair one last tug, Emily crossed to the closet—now jammed with Jessie's clothes—and pulled out her huge beige smock.

"You're wearing *that?*" Jessie exclaimed shrilly.

Emily wriggled, letting the smock fall over her body like a tent. "It's my lucky smock," she replied. She had bought it at a tag sale and had been wearing it ever since. The smock was about five sizes too big. But she felt so comfortable in it. So hidden.

So safe.

She heard the crunch of car tires over snow. Gazing out the window, she saw a blue Honda roll by. Not them. The bright sun glared off the icy street.

4

She shut her eyes and pictured Nancy. Nancy's long, silky copper-red hair, her thin, boyish figure, her green eyes. She tried to remember her older sister in happier times. The Nancy she had grown up with, the Nancy she had confided in, had trusted.

A whole year without her sister. No letters. No phone calls.

She tried to remember Nancy's laugh.

Jessie's voice broke into Emily's thoughts. "Are you scared?"

Emily opened her eyes. She shook her head. "No. Not scared. I mean, Nancy had a breakdown—right? She's got to be okay now. Or else the doctors wouldn't let her come home from the hospital."

"Yeah. Right," Jessie agreed, dropping onto the edge of her bed. "I've never seen your mother so nervous."

"I know. She was up all night cleaning," Emily replied.

"Yeah. I heard her," Jessie murmured softly.

Emily raised her eyes to Jessie's. "You were awake? What were you doing up? The nightmare? Again?"

Jessie nodded.

Emily tsk-tsked. Poor Jessie had started dreaming about Jolie again.

Jessie had her own problems, Emily realized. Her own bad memories. Her own nightmares.

Jolie had been Jessie's friend at Jessie's old school. Jolie died in a camping trip accident. Jessie found her body. Others on the camping trip accused Jessie of murdering her.

"I thought I put Jolie behind me," Jessie confided, her voice breaking. "I don't know why I started dreaming about her again."

Emily crossed the room and placed a hand tenderly on her stepsister's shoulder. "It's because of Nancy," she said softly. "We're all so stressed out about Nancy coming home. It's giving us all nightmares."

They hugged each other.

Then Jessie crossed to the dresser. She picked up the fluted glass perfume bottle and sprayed her throat, then her wrists. The sweet fragrance of peaches and roses floated through the room.

"Whoa. Easy," Emily scolded. "That stuff is expensive."

Emily didn't really care about the cost of the perfume. Her boyfriend, Josh, had given her the perfume—and she wanted the bottle to last forever.

Josh had asked his parents to buy it during their trip to Paris. It was the most wonderful present he had ever given her. *Ma Chérie* read the delicate script on the side of the bottle.

On the card Josh had written, "That means *My Darling.*"

Jessie sprayed herself again. "This is called a French bath," she said, grinning in the mirror at Emily. "You spray on perfume—instead of taking a shower."

Emily gritted her teeth. Jessie is using up half the bottle, she saw.

She suddenly remembered that sharing a room with Jessie wasn't the easiest thing in the world. But she forced herself not to say anything. She didn't want to start an argument just before Nancy arrived.

"Did you get everything out of Nancy's room?" Emily asked, inhaling the sweet perfume fragrance.

Jessie finally set the bottle down. "I'll go check."

A moment later she returned, holding a glass crystal swan. "Look who I forgot. I forgot Grace."

The glass crystal swan was Jessie's favorite possession. She loved it because it reminded her of happy times. Jessie's mother had given her the crystal swan four years ago, on Jessie's thirteenth birthday.

Before her parents' divorce. Before Jolie died.

Jessie named the swan Grace. "Because it's the most graceful creature I've ever seen," she explained.

The glass swan really is beautiful, Emily thought. The winter sunlight slanting through the window caught the crystal and made a rainbow prism across the carpet.

"Where should I put Grace?" Jessie asked, gazing around the cluttered bedroom.

"How about the dresser?" Emily suggested. "She'll look really pretty there next to the perfume bottle."

"Perfect," Jessie agreed. Cradling the swan in both hands, she started toward the dresser.

But the scream from the hallway made her hands fly up.

Emily watched the swan fall. Watched its head break off as it hit the floor.

Watched the delicate glass body shatter as the shrill scream grew louder.

chapter

2

"I'll Pay You Back!"

Emily gazed down at the shards of broken glass glinting around Jessie's feet. "Don't move!" she cried, pointing. "You're barefoot."

Rich burst into the room. "I don't *believe* you!" he yelled at Emily.

Emily stared at her stepbrother. Usually his skin was as pale as Jessie's. But now his face burned red with hurt and anger. He let out another scream, an animal growl of frustration.

"You creep! You rotten creep!" he screamed at Emily.

"Me?" cried Emily. "What did I do?"

"You creep—you told!"

"Told?"

Emily turned to Jessie for help. Kneeling, Jessie carefully picked up the fragments of the glass swan. "You're such a *jerk*, Rich," Jessie muttered angrily. "Look what you made me do!"

Rich ignored her. He stormed up to Emily. "Dad grounded me for last night's party." He jabbed a finger at her. "Thanks to you."

The party. At Steve Arnold's house. Steve's parents were away for the weekend. So he had invited a few friends over. And those friends had invited a few of *their* friends and . . . The evening had quickly turned into a very wild and noisy party.

Emily and Josh hung out there for a while. But none of their friends had shown up. Emily convinced Josh to leave the party around ten.

As they were leaving, they spotted Rich and some of his friends goofing around in the kitchen. Someone had pulled a six-pack of beer out of the back of the fridge and handed a can to Rich. Emily didn't see if Rich had drunk it or not.

"I didn't tell on you," she insisted. "I don't know how Dad found out—"

"Oh, *please!*" Rich cut her off. "Don't bother lying. You were there. You saw me. The next thing I know, Dad grounds me. I can put two and two together."

"I'm surprised!" Jessie chimed in. "Math must be your best subject!"

She dumped the broken glass into the wicker basket under Emily's desk.

"Maybe you can glue it," Emily told her.

"No. Too many pieces," Jessie replied. She glanced at her brother.

"Rich, I swear to you," Emily insisted. "I didn't say anything to your father."

"You're a liar!" Rich shot back. "What am I going

to do?" Rich cried. "I can't believe this. I'm grounded. *Grounded!*"

"Oh, big deal," Jessie said, rolling her eyes. "So you can't go out with your nerdy friends for one night."

"One night?" Rich uttered a shrill laugh. "That's what *you* think. Dad grounded me for *six weeks.* You know what that means? My friends and I can't finish *Night of the Living Eyeballs!*"

"Oh, wow. What a loss," Jessie said sarcastically.

Rich whirled to face his sister. "Shut up, freak!"

Emily agreed with Jessie. The horror movie Rich and his friends had been making *did* look pretty dumb. Emily saw part of it when they taped a scene in front of the house. But Rich was into it big time.

Emily tried to control the anger in her voice. "Rich, I'm sorry. But I don't know who told your dad."

"Listen," Jessie told him, "instead of worrying so much about who told, why don't you shape up? Act a little more grown-up, so Dad won't keep you grounded so long."

Rich ignored his sister. He took a menacing step toward Emily, glaring at her.

Every instinct in Emily's body suddenly told her to back off, stay away, be careful. She'd become supersensitive after what happened last year.

"I'll pay you back," Rich growled at her, his voice shaking. "I'll pay you back, Emily! I never wanted to be in this stupid family in the first place. I'll pay you back for ruining my life!"

He stomped out, slamming the door hard behind him.

Emily dropped down heavily on the edge of her bed. Jessie plopped down beside her.

Neither said a word. What a way to start the day, Emily thought. Especially *this* day.

"I didn't tell on him," Emily said.

"I know."

"You know?" Emily stared at Jessie, surprised. She felt a pang of suspicion. "How do you know?" she asked, her eyes narrowing.

"Because," Jessie told her, reddening, "whenever Rich is totally sure about something, he's always wrong."

"Your brother is one weird guy," Emily murmured, staring at the floor.

"All fourteen-year-olds are weird," Jessie replied.

Emily glanced at the door. She lowered her voice. "Have you seen any of the tapes he rents? Those Clive Barker movies? I couldn't sleep after watching one of those things."

"He *doesn't* sleep," Jessie pointed out. "He's always down in the den staring at the tube."

"Or how about that weird cyberpunk sci-fi stuff he's always reading?" added Emily. "I think it's twisting his brain."

"Believe me, it was already twisted."

Jessie smiled at her, but Emily still felt upset. She couldn't help it.

"What?" Jessie asked.

"I don't know. I feel like now he's going to start plotting to kill me or something. You hear what he

11

said? 'I'll pay you back.' I don't need this, Jess. I really don't."

"Don't worry," Jessie assured her. "He doesn't mean it. He's just stressed out, too. You know, about Nancy."

Maybe Jessie is right, Emily thought. Maybe that's why I'm reacting so strongly to Rich's threats. Because Nancy is coming home.

Jessie stood.

"Wait a minute," Emily cautioned. "There's probably more glass." She pulled a pair of sneakers out of the bottom of her closet and tossed them to Jessie. "I'll vacuum," she said.

"No, I'll do it," Jessie insisted.

Emily smiled. The new Jessie. A year ago Jessie would be nice only when their parents were around to watch.

Emily heard a jangle of tags and the click of tiny paws on the hardwood floor of the hall. She pulled open the door and smiled as Butch, her long-haired dachshund, stuck his long thin snout into the room. He gazed up at Emily with soft brown, questioning eyes.

"Butch!" crooned Emily, bending over. "You sweetheart. You came to comfort me, didn't you? Come here, my little dog."

She reached for the little brown dog, arms open wide. Butch leaped through her arms and trotted toward Jessie's bed.

"No way!" Jessie declared, jumping to her feet. "Back off, Butch. Go to Mommy. Jessie hates you."

"Don't tell him that," Emily said, laughing. "You'll hurt his feelings."

"Good," Jessie cried. "Down!"

Butch ignored her orders. He leaped onto her bed and rolled on his back on her bedspread.

"Nooo!" Jessie wailed. "Now he'll get dog hair all over the bed. I'll have to spend hours with Scotch tape trying to get the stuff off my clothes. And I'll probably get some weird kind of dachshund disease."

"He loves you," Emily told her. "The little traitor. Butch, how come you love Jessie so much more than me? Huh?"

Before Butch could explain, the doorbell rang.

Emily stopped laughing. She stared at Jessie.

"It's Nancy!" Jessie cried. "She's here!"

Emily's heart started pounding.

I guess I *am* scared, she realized. Her legs suddenly felt weak and rubbery.

Jessie started for the door. Emily followed close behind. She almost tripped over Butch as he scooted out the door.

Butch beat them both downstairs. He barked wildly at the front door.

Halfway down the stairs Emily froze.

She watched as Jessie took the stairs two at a time.

Jessie reached for the doorknob.

Emily stared at the front door as if hypnotized.

What will Nancy be like?

chapter

3

Nancy Attacks

Jessie opened the door, letting in a blast of icy air.

"Cora-Ann!" she cried.

Emily smiled and scooped up Butch, who kept barking loudly. She felt relieved—then she felt guilty for feeling relieved.

She liked Cora-Ann. Jessie and Cora-Ann had become very close friends. Sometimes Emily felt envious of how much time Cora-Ann spent with Jessie. But most of the time she enjoyed having Cora-Ann around.

"Did I come at a bad time?" Cora-Ann asked, glancing at Emily and Jessie with a puzzled grin.

"No," Jessie replied awkwardly. "We just thought you were . . . someone else."

Cora-Ann appeared confused. Then she slapped her forehead. "Wait a minute. It's Saturday. The day— You thought I was—Oh, wow, I am so stupid! Emily's

14

sister is coming home today, right? Oh, wow. And I barge in on you."

"You're not barging in," Jessie insisted. She lowered her voice in a mock whisper. "We need you to protect us!"

"Jessie!" Emily scolded her.

When Nancy first went into the hospital, Emily's parents had instructed the family to keep Nancy's breakdown a secret. They were supposed to tell everyone that Nancy had gone to visit relatives in California.

Right, Emily thought. Like anyone would believe that.

As the months dragged on, they had all told more and more people the truth. Emily doubted there was anyone left in Shadyside who didn't know the whole sad story.

"Sure you guys don't want me to go?" Cora-Ann asked. "Really, just say the word."

Emily took Cora-Ann's hand. "March," she ordered, leading her up the stairs.

When they reached the top of the stairs, Emily couldn't help glancing down the hall to Rich's room. The door was closed. She felt a shiver of panic.

He hates me.

"Oh, wow!" Cora-Ann exclaimed as she came into Emily's cluttered bedroom. "Guess you two are going to be real close!"

"We don't mind!" Jessie answered quickly, glancing at Emily. "Here, let me hang your coat up for you." She took Cora-Ann's blue parka—and dropped it on the floor.

"Thanks, pal," Cora-Ann said. Cora-Ann never got angry, no matter what Jessie did to her. No wonder Jessie liked her so much!

Emily hung up the coat. "Jessie, now that we're rooming together, I want to show you where the closet is. See?"

"Just cause I'm not a neat freak like you and your mom—" Jessie began.

"You two aren't really fighting, are you?" Cora-Ann asked.

"No way," Emily assured her. "You'll know when we really fight. That's when we start punching each other out."

Cora-Ann blushed.

Jessie shot Emily a sharp look.

Bad joke, Emily realized. Cora-Ann's parents were always battling—for real. Which explained why she'd been spending so much time at the Wallner house.

Cora-Ann perched on the edge of Emily's bed. "You're totally sure this isn't a bad time?"

Emily wished Cora-Ann wasn't always so eager to please. Cora-Ann was fun and cute with her short auburn hair and glasses. But she acted as if anyone who wanted to spend time with her was doing her a big favor.

"Cora-Ann," Jessie replied, "you don't have to keep asking that. It's always okay for you to come over. Always."

Well, not *always*, thought Emily.

"Oh, I was going to call you, Jess!" Cora-Ann announced. "Guess who Annette Holloway went to the Division Street Mall with last night?"

"Who?" Emily and Jessie asked in unison.

Cora-Ann smiled, keeping them in suspense. "Teddy Miller. Do you believe it?"

"No!" gasped Jessie. "What's with her?"

"I don't know. I mean, she told me she's still not over Pete Goodwin."

Emily sat at her desk and opened the top drawer. "Hey, what happened to my supplies?"

"Oh," Jessie said from her bed. "I switched your stuff to the lower drawer because you have the top bookshelf. It's only fair."

"Great," Emily grumbled. She didn't really mind. Jessie was still Jessie. But so what? Emily suddenly felt in a great mood. "Sit back," she told Cora-Ann. "You look so tense. You're making me nervous."

"What? Oh. Okay." Cora-Ann leaned back, but she sat up again a second later.

Emily found a bag of Oreos in the bottom drawer. She tossed a cookie to Cora-Ann.

"Wow, thanks!" Cora-Ann gushed.

She's always so grateful for any little thing, Emily thought. It sort of breaks your heart.

"Mmm," Cora-Ann said. She cupped her hand underneath the cookie to catch the crumbs. "Hey, want me to go down and get some juice or milk?"

"You're not the maid," Jessie answered sharply. "Emily, go get the milk."

They all laughed.

"So what about Teddy Miller?" Emily demanded.

"I'm getting to that. Last night Annette was supposed to go to some party at Steve Arnold's."

"Emily went to that party," Jessie interrupted.

"You did?" Cora-Ann asked, wide-eyed. "I heard the police came and broke it up around midnight."

I knew that would happen, Emily thought. I'm so glad Josh and I left early.

"So get to the part about Teddy," Jessie urged.

"I am," insisted Cora-Ann. "Last night Pete was there with there with one of Annette's friends."

Jessie studied a strand of hair for split ends. "Pete is such a loser," she murmured. "I'm surprised *I* haven't gone out with him!"

"That reminds me!" cried Cora-Ann, clapping. "I think I found a guy for you to double with me and Michael next Saturday night."

"Whoa. Wait a minute!" cried Emily. "You still haven't told us about Teddy!"

"I'm getting to that," Cora-Ann insisted. They all laughed, getting half-hysterical. It always took Cora-Ann so long to tell a simple story.

"Emily," Jessie said, "open the window, okay? This room is like a sauna."

"What am I? Your slave?" Emily asked. But she jumped up and opened the window. The blast of icy air felt great, even though the cold wind blew right through her thin muslin smock.

"Anyway," Cora-Ann resumed her story. "Annette was feeling really annoyed about Pete. So when Teddy called her to ask her out for like the hundred millionth time, this time she said yes. Lisa Blume claims she saw them parking at the mall and making out like crazy."

Jessie made puking sounds. "Gross! I'd rather kiss Emily's dog."

"Oh, come on," Emily protested. "Butch isn't that bad."

That got them all laughing.

They stopped at once when they heard the familiar crunch of tires as Mr. Wallner's car pulled into the snowy driveway.

Emily heard a scrabble of toenails on wood, and a moment later, the *thump-thumping* sound as Butch hurried down the front stairs.

Emily turned and glanced down at the driveway. She saw her mother opening the passenger's side door. Caught a glimpse of Nancy beside her. Two heads of identical shiny copper-colored hair. Beautiful, like fire.

"She's here!" Emily told them. For some reason she whispered.

"Want me to stay up here in the room?" Cora-Ann demanded.

Emily shook her head. "No way. Come on. You're pretty much a part of our family now anyway. I want Nancy to meet you."

Emily led the way out the door.

Down the stairs.

The front door opened.

Emily stopped short. Jessie and Cora-Ann bumped into her from behind.

19

"Hi!" Mrs. Wallner smiled up at them, too broadly. "Hi, Emily. Hi, Jessie, Hi—Oh, hi, Cora-Ann . . . it's so nice of you to drop by."

Emily could always tell when her mother was nervous. She got extra polite.

Mr. Wallner entered behind her, pulling the black ski cap off his bald head. "That railing is loose again," he grumbled to Emily's mother. "I tell those kids not to sit on it, but do they listen?" He looked up at them. "Oh, hi."

Emily, Jessie, and Cora-Ann were all downstairs now. Emily tried to see past Mr. Wallner. She couldn't stand the tension any longer. "Where's Nancy?" she cried.

Mr. Wallner had left the front door open behind him.

Now Nancy stepped inside.

Emily froze.

Nancy appeared so strange, so dazed.

She lurched into the house, her eyes wide.

"No!" Emily let out a cry as she saw the blood-stained knife in Nancy's hand.

chapter
4

A Bad Spill

Nancy raised the knife.

Emily gasped and staggered back against Jessie.

"I found this by the hedge," Nancy said, narrowing her eyes. She glanced back out the open door. "What was it doing out there?"

"By the hedge?" Mr. Wallner cried. He reached for it. "Let me see that."

Emily covered her mouth. She felt embarrassed that she had cried out. She could feel her ears burning.

Cora-Ann peered over Mr. Wallner's shoulder. Then she laughed. "Oh, I know what it is. It's a prop from *Night of the Living Eyeballs.*"

"From *what?*" Mr. Wallner demanded, studying the knife.

"That's Rich's horror movie," Jessie explained. "The one he and his friends are taping for school."

"*Were* taping," Mr. Wallner corrected her. "That

21

kid . . . Believe me, Nancy, I'll put a stop to that. I'm very sorry. What a welcome home."

Nancy smiled, a slight, crooked smile. "Don't be sorry. Not on my account anyway. It's no problem. Really."

She's speaking much more softly than she used to, Emily thought. It made her heart ache. And Nancy had gotten thinner. She seemed lost inside her blue down coat.

Emily pushed past her stepfather. "Nancy!" She threw her arms out wide and hugged her.

Nancy didn't really hug her back, just stood there, as if giving in to the hug.

"I missed you so much," Emily whispered in her ear.

Nancy smiled at her but didn't say anything. What had they done to her in that place? Emily wondered, horrified.

"Hi, Nance," said Jess, with a little wave. She stuck out her hand, but then changed her mind and hugged Nancy as well.

Their mother hugged Nancy.

"Mom," Nancy said quietly, "we did this at the hospital. Remember?"

Everyone laughed.

Emily's stepfather still held the bloody knife.

"Oh, Hugh, why don't you throw that thing out?" her mother demanded.

"Good idea." He stepped out the front door, shaking his head. He came back inside carrying Nancy's white canvas overnight bag.

"Nance," Jessie said. "I want you to meet Cora-Ann Haver."

Cora-Ann stepped forward, blushing shyly. "I'm sorry," she apologized. "I didn't mean to barge in on your homecoming. I just—I forgot today was the day, actually, and—"

Nancy smiled. "Hey," she replied. "I appreciate it. Gives me a bigger welcome-home party."

"Oh," Cora-Ann said, "that's so sweet of you to say. You're right, Em," she added, turning to Emily, "your sister is great!"

Emily couldn't remember telling Cora-Ann any such thing. She was glad that Cora-Ann had said it, though.

Nancy, however, did not react. She stared blankly. Emily thought maybe she was on overload from all the attention.

Cora-Ann squealed. "Nancy, I like your earrings!"

Nancy pulled her straight coppery hair to the side, showing off a small seashell earring. "Made it myself," she said proudly.

But then her expression went blank again.

Emily's heart sank. Her mom had said Nancy was better.

Of course, she had also warned her—and warned her and warned her—not to expect too much of Nancy when she first came home.

"Give her time," Mrs. Wallner told Emily again and again.

Even so . . . .

It seemed as if Nancy was just going through the

motions. Pretending to be social. She appeared so pale, so lifeless, so withdrawn.

Nancy finally seemed to notice Butch, yipping at her heels. She bent down to pet him. He immediately collapsed onto his back, paws in the air, waiting for her to scratch his belly.

"That's Butch," Emily told her. "I think he likes you."

Nancy smiled. "Feeling's mutual."

Nancy seemed to focus on Emily for the first time. "Hi, Em," she said softly.

Emily melted. All of a sudden Nancy was back. Emily grinned. "Hi."

They hugged all over again. Then, arm in arm, they turned to face the rest of the group.

"Now that's a scene I like to see," Mr. Wallner announced, beaming. "One happy family."

Emily heard her mom sob. Everyone turned to her in surprise. "Sorry," Mrs. Wallner said, hunting in her purse for a tissue. "I'm just—"

"Well," Jessie said, checking her watch, "she lasted two minutes twenty-nine seconds without crying. You win the bet, Emily."

Everyone laughed, including Mrs. Wallner, who laughed while blowing her nose.

"Where is Rich?" Mr. Wallner asked, frowning. "He ought to be down here." He gazed up the stairs.

"Hugh"—Mrs. Wallner placed one hand on her husband's arm—"don't start."

"Well, where is he?"

"Sulking in his room," Jessie said. "You grounded him, remember?"

"I'll do more than that if he doesn't come down right away. His stepsister comes home after a year, and he stays in his room." Mr. Wallner shook his head. "No sense!"

"Hugh . . ." Emily's mother warned.

"Don't worry. I won't start up with him. Rich!" he called. "Nancy's here. Come down here, Scout."

"Dad," Jessie groaned. "He's fourteen."

"So?"

"You called him Scout when he was seven and in the Cub Scouts."

"Well, that's about how old he's been acting," Mr. Wallner grumbled. He crossed to the foot of the stairs and put one hand on the banister. "Rich, come down here this second or you're grounded for *twelve* weeks. Understand? I'm going to count. Five. Four."

A door slammed upstairs. A moment later Rich appeared at the top of the stairs. They all watched him saunter down, hands in his jeans pockets. He brushed past Emily, deliberately bumping into her.

"Hey," she protested.

He turned and gave Emily a big smile. Emily thought it looked more like he was baring his teeth.

"Hi," he told Nancy, taking one hand out of his pocket to wave at her. "How's it going?"

"Not bad," Nancy replied, with that same half-smile she'd been giving everyone.

There was an awkward pause. Rich flashed Emily

another angry look. Then he turned and started back toward the stairs.

Mr. Wallner clapped a hand on his shoulder. "Where do you think you're going?" he demanded.

"Back to my room," Rich answered.

"Are you insane? Your sister just got home."

Insane. Great choice of words, thought Emily, wincing.

Mr. Wallner noticed everyone staring at him. "What?" he demanded.

"Hey, Rich," Cora-Ann said, "I just remembered. I watched a movie on cable last night, and I wanted to ask you about it. It was called *Gnaw.* About giant rats. You ever see that one?"

Go, Cora-Ann! thought Emily, grateful to Jessie's friend for saving the day once again.

Rich's mouth dropped open. "You like horror?" he asked Cora-Ann suspiciously.

"I love it," Cora-Ann gushed.

Rich nodded. "What's your favorite horror movie?"

Uh-oh, thought Emily. He's testing her. She hoped that Cora-Ann wasn't just being polite when she said she liked horror because—

"Uh . . . *The Shining* I guess," Cora-Ann replied. "Did you read the book? It was even scarier than the movie."

"Hey, cool," Rich said. He grinned. She'd passed the test.

Maybe I'll tell Jessie to invite Cora-Ann to stay here

26

permanently, Emily thought. And not just on the nights when her parents are tearing each other apart.

"Hey, Nance," Emily said. "Aren't you going to admire my beautiful outfit?"

She lifted the hem of her huge smock, twirling like a model. She waited for Nancy to make some cutting remark. The old Nancy would have.

But all her sister said was, "Very nice."

Emily felt a chill. She exchanged a worried glance with Jessie.

"Well," Nancy told them, reaching for her canvas bag, "I guess I'd better go unpack."

Everyone stepped forward at once, reaching for the bag, offering to take it upstairs for her.

Nancy laughed. "That's okay. I can manage just fine."

She started up the stairs. Everyone watched her go. She turned halfway up and smiled again.

"Don't worry," Nancy insisted. "I'm fine. I'm just so stressed out from all the excitement. You know, coming home. I think I need to set up my room. Unpack. I'll be fine. I promise."

Everyone spoke up again, promising her that they knew she would be fine, and of course, she should go and relax. That kind of thing. We're tripping all over ourselves, Emily thought.

Nancy smiled her half-smile, then turned and climbed the rest of the way up the stairs. Alone. Everyone watched her.

"Well," Mr. Wallner said loudly after she was gone. "That went well." He smiled happily.

How wrong could he be? Emily wondered. He has to be the most insensitive man in the universe!

Mr. Wallner clapped his hands. "Okay. I'm going to go watch the end of the Bears game. You all—"

"We'll all do whatever, Hugh," Mrs. Wallner interrupted him. "Don't worry about us."

He shrugged. "I'm not worrying. You're the one who's worrying. Where are you going?"

"To prepare your dinner, of course," she answered, sighing. She headed into the dining room as Mr. Wallner made his way to the den.

She's even more nervous than I realized, Emily thought.

Rich flashed Emily one last threatening glare, then took the steps back to his room two at a time.

"Hey, Cora-Ann," Jessie said, tugging on her friend's sleeve. "I want to show you a new way I learned to put on eyeliner." She led her friend up the stairs.

Cora-Ann is like her toy doll, Emily observed. Or maybe I'm jealous of how close they are.

Emily stood all alone in the foyer. She held on to the banister, trying to get her bearings. Trying to absorb the fact that Nancy was home.

She felt a little let down. She'd been thinking about this moment for so long—fearing it, longing for it. And now it had come and gone.

She could hear Nancy moving around in her room upstairs. Emily's heart leaped. Nancy! Nancy was home! She wanted to race up and see her, tackle her, tickle her, hug her.

But maybe I'd better give her some time alone, Emily thought. That's what Nancy wants.

She went into the kitchen instead. Mrs. Wallner stood by the sink, her back to Emily.

"Hey," Emily said.

Her mother turned. Her eyes were red with tears. She reached for the paper towel roll and blew her nose loudly on the rough paper.

"Don't use that," Emily said. "I'll get tissues."

"I'm sorry." Mrs. Wallner wiped her eyes.

"Don't be sorry. What are you sorry about?"

"It's just—I'm so glad she's home!"

"Oh, right. You look really glad." Emily rolled her eyes. "I'm glad too," she added. She knew that would make her mom happy.

"Oh, sweetheart . . ." Mrs. Wallner came toward her and held her face with both hands. "You mean that?"

Why couldn't her mother stop worrying? Why couldn't she ever believe anything anyone said?

"No, I'm lying to you. Like always," Emily replied. "Of course I mean it, Mom."

Mrs. Wallner sniffed. "Em? I know this is going to be hard on you. But—"

"But we have to do everything we can to make Nancy feel comfortable and at home," Emily finished the speech for her. She'd heard it often enough these past few weeks.

"That's right," Mrs. Wallner agreed.

"Mom, I know this doesn't mean much. But don't worry, okay? She's better. She's back. We're a family again." Emily kissed her mother's cheek. "Everything's going to be fine. I promise."

Mrs. Wallner grinned and wiped her eyes again.

Emily headed back into the front hall. She could hear her stepfather yelling at the players in the football game on TV. Sounded as if the Bears were losing.

She made her way upstairs. She could hear Nancy moving around in her room. Down the hall, Rich's door was closed, as usual. At the other end of the hall, in her parents' room, Emily heard Jessie and Cora-Ann giggling over something. She could see them standing in front of Mrs. Wallner's makeup mirror.

Emily sniffed. A familiar, but powerful scent filled the air. The smell of peaches and roses.

Strange. Had Jessie been—?

Emily started toward the open door to her room.

The aroma grew stronger.

Emily stopped in the doorway—and gasped.

Her perfume bottle.

Her precious *Ma Chérie* perfume.

The bottle lay open. On its side.

The perfume poured down the front of the dresser, making a dark puddle on the carpet.

chapter
5

Strangled

"Who did this? *Who?*" Emily shrieked.

She heard the thump and clatter of people running down the hall.

Jessie and Cora-Ann dived into the room. "What's wrong?" Jessie asked breathlessly.

"Look." Emily motioned to the dresser and the spilled perfume.

"Uh-oh," Jessie murmured. She quickly stepped forward and set the fluted bottle upright.

"There's no point," Emily said, sighing. "She spilled it all."

"Who did?" Cora-Ann asked, her dark eyes wide.

"Nancy, of course," Emily snapped. "Who do you think?"

She saw the glances Cora-Ann and Jessie exchanged. I'm not the crazy one, Emily thought. Nancy is home for two minutes and the trouble starts again.

"Emily, look, the window." Jessie instructed.

Emily turned. The window was still raised, the cold icy wind lifting the curtains. "You left the window open," Jessie said. "Remember?"

"So?" Emily demanded.

"Sooo," Jessie said, "the wind probably blew the perfume over."

She sounds the way I do when I'm trying to explain something to Butch, Emily thought unhappily. "No way," Emily insisted, shaking her head. But she felt her anger fading.

"I'm going to talk to Nancy." Emily started out of the room, but Jessie blocked her way. Emily saw Cora-Ann's eyes narrow with concern.

"Don't," Jessie said sternly. "Mom and Dad will massacre you if you accuse Nancy of something now. She *just* got home!"

"Yeah, really. Calm down, Em," Cora-Ann pleaded. "I mean, are you going to blame Nancy for every accident that happens?"

Emily suddenly felt about a hundred pounds heavier. She dropped down on the edge of her bed.

"I don't know what's wrong with me." She sighed. "I was about to do something really stupid, wasn't I?"

They nodded.

"An accident," Emily muttered, shaking her head. She wanted to believe it was an accident. She really did.

"Wow!" cried a voice at the door.

Emily glanced up.

Rich stood in the doorway sniffing the air. He made a disgusted face. "Gross. What stinks in here?"

Rich. She hadn't even stopped to think it might be Rich.

"I'll pay you back!" he had shouted.

Now Emily stared hard at him. "Did you do it, Rich?" she demanded. "Did you?"

A grin slowly spread over his face. "Maybe," he replied.

The next morning, a Sunday morning, Emily slept late. She woke up to the sound of her stepfather yelling cheerfully up the stairs. "Everybody, up and at 'em! Come on—rise and shine!"

To Emily's surprise, he planned to take them to the new waffle and pancake house that had opened on Division Street. Mr. Wallner had grumbled all year about how bad business was at the furniture factory where he was manager. And money had been tight at home.

But today was a day to celebrate. The family was back together. A big, noisy pancake house was the perfect way to celebrate their reunion.

Emily hurried to get dressed. She pulled a bright yellow sweater down over black leggings. She wanted to look cheerful and festive.

"Hey, Rich—get going. Rich, where are you?" She could hear her stepfather calling in the hall.

No reply from her stepbrother's room.

"Hey, Rich—?" Mr. Wallner practically pleading.

Finally a sullen reply through Rich's closed bedroom door: "I'm not going. I'm grounded—remember?"

And so they drove off without him. Emily's mother and stepfather in the front seat of the four-year-old Taurus. The three girls squeezed in the back, chattering away as if they'd just met.

They ordered pancakes and eggs. Mr. Wallner ordered a tall stack of pancakes with eggs and a steak on top. When it arrived, he drowned it all in butter and maple syrup.

He's so gross, Emily thought. He's trying to be a good sport, but he's just so gross. As he leaned over his plate, his bald head shone in the bright overhead lights.

"Mmmmm. Best meal I've had in a year!" Nancy exclaimed. She had a spot of syrup on her chin. "You know, I actually dreamed about pancakes one night. I really did!"

"I dreamed I was eating a peanut butter sandwich the other night," Jessie offered.

"Crunchy or smooth?" Nancy demanded.

"Crunchy. Definitely crunchy," Jessie replied. "When I woke up, my teeth hurt."

It wasn't that funny, but everyone laughed.

Nancy seems a lot more like herself this morning, Emily thought happily.

"Know what you call a waffle that was made with spoiled eggs?" Mr. Wallner chimed in, his mouth full of food.

Nancy played along. "No. What?"

"An *awful waffle!*"

The girls all groaned. "That's pitiful, Dad!" Emily exclaimed. She had decided to call her stepfather Dad a few months earlier. It was starting to feel natural.

Emily's mom laughed. Her eyes sparkled.

Emily couldn't believe her mother really enjoyed his terrible jokes. She really loves the guy, Emily realized. Even after more than a year, that could still surprise Emily.

Emily saw her stepfather's smile fade. "I just wish Rich would shape up," he said, scowling. "He should be here with us." He tossed his napkin onto the table. "I'm kind of worried about Rich."

Me, too, Emily thought. Me, too.

Emily jumped when she felt a hand on her wrist. She turned to find Nancy smiling at her.

"When we get home, let's have a long talk," Nancy suggested. "I was too tired last night. There's so much to catch up on."

"That would be great!" Emily agreed happily. "I— I've missed talking to you so much."

She saw her mother smiling across the table at them.

Things are definitely looking up, Emily thought.

Breakfast lasted nearly two hours. The longest— and noisiest—family breakfast Emily could remember.

When they finally returned home, Nancy and Emily slipped off to the den. The shades were drawn. The room was dark.

Rich must have been up late, watching horror

movies again, Emily thought. He always liked to pull the shades and make the room into a cave.

Emily fumbled for the light switch.

But before she could reach it, she felt Nancy's hands slide around her throat.

Emily uttered a choked gasp—as Nancy began to strangle her.

chapter
6

Roar

"Ohhh . . ." A low moan escaped Emily's lips.

She staggered back.

Nancy quickly let go.

For a moment Emily felt too stunned to move. Then she scrambled back, her hand clawing the paneled wall. She staggered into something—the couch.

The lights flashed on.

Nancy stood in the den doorway, calmly staring at Emily.

"Why did you do that?" Emily choked out, rubbing her neck with both hands. "What do you think you're doing?" Her heart pounded. Her voice came out breathless and shrill.

Nancy brushed back her coppery hair. "I'm sorry, Em. I had to prove a point."

"Huh? A point?" Emily shrieked. "By strangling me?"

"When I touched your arm in the restaurant, you jumped a mile," Nancy said softly, calmly.

"Yes. Well—"

"I didn't know what to expect when I got back home," Nancy continued, leaning against the doorframe, her green eyes locked on Emily. "I figured you probably hadn't forgiven me. But I didn't expect you to jump out of your skin whenever I touched your arm."

"Nancy—you—you just tried to *choke* me!" Emily sputtered.

Nancy shook her head. "No, I didn't. I put my hands on your neck. But I didn't squeeze. I didn't try to choke you. But you—you're *terrified* of me." Nancy's voice broke. "I—I didn't expect that."

Emily took a few hesitant steps toward her sister. "You scared me, that's all. I'm not terrified. Really. But pretending to strangle me is no way to prove that—"

"I just wanted to show you how frightened you are," Nancy insisted. She narrowed her eyes thoughtfully. "Look, I don't blame you for being scared. But here's the thing. I'm okay now. And I will never—ever—try to hurt you again. So now you have to promise me you won't be afraid of me. Because—"

Her voice caught. She waited a moment. "Because . . . it hurts too much."

Nancy sighed. Tears rolled down her pale cheeks. "It's okay to cry," she said softly. "It's good to cry.

Feelings are good. Not bad. Feelings are nothing to be ashamed of." She smiled. "Doctor talk," she explained.

"Oh, I see," Emily responded, feeling uncomfortable.

"You believe me, don't you?" Nancy asked. "You can see I'm better, can't you?"

Emily wanted to believe her. But then, why had she used such a violent way to prove her point?

Emily shoved the question from her mind. She smiled. "I believe you."

Nancy wiped away the tears. "Come on, let's go up to my room so we can really talk. This room depresses me.

"You still going out with Josh?" Nancy asked as they climbed the stairs.

She asked it so casually, as if she were asking Emily the time of day. Nancy had gone out with Josh first, before Emily.

"Yeah," Emily answered, trying to sound just as casual, "still going out with him.

"Wow," Emily said, entering Nancy's room. "It's starting to look like—like it used to."

The week before, their mother had spent hours moving all of Nancy's collections—beads and dolls and other stuff—down from the attic. Yesterday she had put them back on the long shelves that lined one wall. Nancy had moved her furniture back where it always had been.

Nancy plopped down on the cane rocking chair. She watched Emily as Emily walked around the room.

"What's that sheet on the wall?" Emily asked.

"It's covering my mural. I started it early this morning."

"Your *mural?* You're painting the wall? Does Mom know?"

"Mom said I could do whatever I wanted. That's one of the little benefits of cracking up, Emily. Once you've gone really nuts, everyone bends over backward to be nice to you. You should try it."

Emily laughed. "So what's it a mural of?" she asked, picking up one corner of the sheet.

"Hey—no way!" Nancy leaned forward and snatched the sheet away. "No peeking till it's done. All I can tell you is it's going to be a big picture that will express all my feelings. Oh, and look what I found."

She held up some college bulletins. "I figure it's time for me to reapply."

College. That sounded so normal. Emily began to feel really hopeful. If Nancy really was herself again, they had a long life ahead of them. A long life as sisters.

"That's great. You sure you're ready for college?" she asked, careful not to make her question sound critical.

"If I get in, I'll wait a year—to give myself more time to recuperate. You know."

Emily nodded. "Sure."

All year Emily had imagined this scene in her mind. She and Nancy finally confronting each other. Sometimes she'd pictured herself crying, sometimes shouting. She had never imagined that they'd be chatting so calmly.

"How are Mom and Hugh getting along?" Nancy asked. "Come on, I want to hear the dirt. They're not still all lovey-dovey, are they?"

"Afraid so."

"That's so cute!" Nancy exclaimed, her eyes twinkling.

They both giggled.

"And how are you getting along with Jessie these days?" Nancy asked.

"Jessie? We're—" Emily stopped herself. Wow, nice going, she told herself. She had almost started raving about how close she and Jessie had become.

"Getting along?" Nancy prompted.

"Pretty much," Emily said.

"I think it's amazing you two are getting along at all, considering everything I did to turn you against her," Nancy commented.

She said it matter-of-factly, but then she gave Emily a guilty smile. A smile filled with pain.

It must be so hard for Nancy to forgive herself, Emily thought. Emily felt terribly sorry for Nancy all of a sudden.

Nancy leaned her head back and looked straight up at the ceiling. Emily found herself admiring her sister's profile, the thin straight nose, just like Mom's, the red hair falling gently around her shoulders. Nancy gazed back down at her and smiled.

"What?" asked Emily.

"That stain on the ceiling. It's still there."

Emily glanced up and laughed. Once, years ago, she and Nancy had filled their water pistols with root beer, figuring it would be a fun way to drink the soda. They'd ended up having a wild water pistol fight instead.

"Dad was so furious," Emily remembered, laughing. "I'd never seen him so angry."

"He had just finished replastering the ceiling in here after that leak in the attic," Nancy remembered.

Nancy turned. Their eyes met. Emily felt totally relaxed.

It was more than that. Mom and Nancy were the only ones who shared Emily's memories of her father. Now that Nancy was back, she felt as if she had a little bit of her father back, too.

"Nance," she said softly, feeling a lump in her throat. "I'm glad you're back."

Nancy frowned. "You're afraid to ask, aren't you? You don't have to be. I'm not made out of glass."

Emily made a face. "Afraid to ask what?"

Nancy imitated Emily's voice. "So, Nance. How was the hospital?"

"Oh. Yeah. How was it?"

They both laughed.

"You want to know something crazy?" Nancy asked. She smiled. "In a lot of ways, the hospital was great."

"It was?" After every weekend visit their mother made to the hospital, she had assured Emily that

Nancy was being treated well. She said it was a fancy, well-run place. Not like the mental hospitals in the movies.

But no matter how hard Emily tried, she couldn't stop picturing Nancy going through the worst tortures.

"Really? How was it great?" she asked.

"Everything is taken care of for you, Em. Every day there's a schedule. And there are a lot of activities. Clay sculpting. Painting. Storytelling sessions. Wood shop. Even car repair."

"That does sound good," Emily replied. "Maybe I should go."

Nancy chuckled. "Well, there's a point to all those activities, of course. It's supposed to help you work out your anger."

"Oh."

Nancy gazed down at her hands. Emily noticed her torn, ragged fingernails. Nancy used to take such good care of her nails, Emily thought.

Nancy folded her hands. "I should never have blamed you, Em." Her face creased with guilt. "That was so—well, it was insane, is what it was."

Emily swallowed hard. "You blamed me for Dad's death. Hey, I blamed myself for that, too. I still do."

"Well, don't!" Nancy cried, her voice rising. "Blame is poison. Pure poison. Dad died in a horrible accident. You happened to be there. End of story."

Except that wasn't the end of the story, thought Emily, feeling about to cry.

She had been on the powerboat with her dad when

it capsized. She had watched him drown right in front of her eyes.

And then she had watched him drown again and again and again in her thoughts and memories and dreams.

It must have been the same for Nancy. And her anger had driven her mad.

"That's what I've learned to accept," Nancy was telling her. "Sometimes bad things just happen. Bad things happened to us. But the doctors showed me how my anger was totally misdirected. I was mad at the universe. It's kind of hard to get your revenge on the universe. So I picked you instead."

"I think I understand," Emily answered.

Nancy gave her a hopeful smile. "But here's the good news. Now my anger is all gone and . . ." Nancy's voice sounded tiny. "And I hope that someday you'll forgive me."

Emily nodded. "I already do."

Nancy shook her head. "You don't have to say that."

"But I do, Nance. I forgive you."

Nancy studied her face. Her eyes watered over.

Emily glanced up at the clock. "Oh, no! I'm totally late. I was supposed to meet Josh twenty minutes ago!"

Nancy followed her to the door, then put a hand on her arm. "Thanks, Em. Thanks for being so understanding."

Suddenly the den door swung open and Butch ran

in. He started barking, jumping up, putting his little paws on their legs, wanting to be included.

"Look who's here!" Nancy cried, laughing, delighted.

Emily picked up Butch so that he could lick Nancy's face. She laughed. His body hung down from her hands like a long furry sausage.

"This is your aunt Nancy, Butchie," Emily announced in a baby voice. "That's right. Give her a kiss."

Nancy giggled, trying to pull her head back. But Butch worked his way out of Emily's grasp and climbed into Nancy's arms. He squirmed as he licked her cheek and neck. Nancy kissed the dog's nose. "Thank you, Butch," she crooned. "You really know how to make me feel like part of the family again."

"Okay, now I'm going to do a triple axel, then spin you into a quadruple lutz. You land on one skate and—"

"Josh, no! Do not spin me. Do not!"

Emily shrieked as Josh spun her anyway. She felt the metal blades of her skates lock together.

She started to fall. Josh tried to hold her up.

They both went down together. They slid along the ice.

Then lay still.

"You okay?" he asked finally.

"You mean, except for the broken ribs?" She rolled over onto her back with a groan.

45

"I'm sorry," he said, breathing hard.

"Sorry?" she groaned. "That's what you said the last three times you spun me down onto the ice."

He laughed. "All right, I'm not sorry." He turned so that his face touched hers.

Now *she* wasn't sorry. She loved his curly, black hair and dark eyes.

Fear Lake lay deep in the heart of the Fear Street woods, far away from the rest of the world.

The two of them, on the glittering ice of the frozen lake. All alone under the clear blue December sky. Perfect.

Except for the fact that Emily could barely skate.

"I'm not getting up this time," Emily told him.

Josh's eyes gleamed. "Good," he declared. Then he kissed her.

It wasn't their greatest kiss of all time. For one thing, both their noses were running.

"So how's Nancy doing?" Josh asked, scissoring his skates back and forth so they scraped the ice.

Emily couldn't help feeling a twinge of jealousy whenever Josh asked about her sister.

She pushed the jealous thoughts away. "I think she's pretty good. Considering, you know. I guess it'll take us a while before we really know each other again. But—"

"But?"

She shrugged. "But I'm excited. To have her back." She sat up. "She's painting a mural on her bedroom wall."

Josh climbed back to his feet gracefully and easily. He reached down to help her up. Her legs slid out from under her. They almost fell over again.

"What's it of?" he asked, helping her steady herself.

"What's what of? Oh, the mural? I don't know. Nancy won't show me. She won't show anyone until it's finished."

Emily shivered, picturing the white sheet that Nancy had taped over the wall. After everything that had happened, Emily had come to hate surprises.

"Okay," Josh said, pushing off with one skate, "let's head back." He skated backward. "Come on. You look frozen."

She didn't argue. She managed to make it back to the edge of the pond without falling.

Great. Soon she'd be ready for the Olympics.

They sat on two big rocks as they pulled off the skates and tugged on their hiking boots. Then they started through the snowy woods toward Emily's house.

They were nearly to Fear Street when Emily heard a high-pitched whine. Like someone chopping down trees with a power saw.

The whine grew louder.

She gazed across the snow to see three dirt bikers roar toward them.

They were tearing up the woods, each bike sending up a spray of powdery snow.

Josh and Emily both froze. The bikers turned, as if aiming at them.

Closer.

Closer.

They're not going to stop. They're coming right at us! Emily realized.

Then she let out a cry of shock.

chapter
7

Up to Her Old Tricks

"**R**ich!" Emily shouted.

Rich braked sharply. His bike slid to a stop inches in front of her. He pulled his snow goggles up onto his forehead and glared at her.

Rich's friends stopped behind him. They sat on their bikes, brooding, staring into the woods. Their goggles looked like evil masks. But Emily recognized the long brown hair of Rich's friend Willy.

"Rich!" Emily cried. "What are you doing?"

"Riding my bike," Rich shot back nastily. "What does it look like I'm doing?" Suddenly he snapped his head forward, barking at her like a dog. She couldn't help it. She gasped.

Rich laughed as if he had just made the world's most hysterical joke.

"Hey, Josh," Rich said, gunning his motor.

"Hey," Josh replied, staring back coldly.

Emily felt so glad Josh was here. Rich was getting to be really weird. Maybe she should hire Josh as a full-time bodyguard.

"Rich," she began, trying to sound as friendly as possible, "I'm not trying to get on your case, okay? But—" She lowered her voice, glancing at his friends. "You're grounded, remember? If your dad finds out—"

"I suppose you're going to tell him, huh, snitch?" Rich said, sneering. "My sister is a Spy. She tells my dad everything I do," he explained to his friends.

He turned back to Emily. "If you tell him this time, Emily, I promise you—"

"You promise her what?" Josh asked. Emily saw fear flicker in Rich's eyes.

"She'll regret it, that's all," Rich answered. He lowered his voice and leaned close to Emily. "I've already warned you," he said.

Emily made a face. "Oh, would you stop acting like such a tough guy? We live together, remember? I know you, Rich. You're not really like this. Let's try to be friends, okay?"

Rich didn't answer. He sneered again. Then he gunned the motor and roared away.

She turned. Josh gave her a shrug. "What a jerk," he muttered.

"Josh, I'm really worried about him."

Josh started walking on ahead. "Don't be," he told her without glancing back. She had to hurry to catch up.

"Why not?"

He didn't answer.

"Seriously. Why shouldn't I be worried? He never talks to anyone except his creepy friends. He fights with his father all the time. He gets into all kinds of trouble. And now he's got it in his head that *I'm* the cause of all his problems."

"He's fourteen," Josh said, as if that explained everything.

"So?"

"Fourteen is a bad year when you're a guy."

"Oh, so now it's a guy thing? That's a whole lot of baloney. Rich was like this last year, when he was thirteen."

"Yeah? Well, thirteen is another bad year for guys. I was like him when I was thirteen."

Emily laughed. But she still felt worried. And a little frightened by Rich and his threats.

Back at Emily's house they made hot cocoa and snuggled together on the leather couch in the den. Emily forgot all about Rich. And Nancy. And everybody else, except Josh.

He pulled her face to his and kissed her.

Emily pulled her head away sharply.

"Huh?" Josh cried.

She stared past Josh to the door.

Someone was standing outside the den door. Emily was sure of it!

"Let me up," she whispered.

Josh released her. She climbed quickly to her feet.

Now she could make out the shadow of someone's feet under the door.

Someone was there. Someone was spying on them!

Nancy!

Was Nancy up to her old tricks after all?

Her heart pounding, Emily tiptoed to the den door and pulled it open.

chapter

8

Falling for Nancy

"Cora-Ann!" Emily cried.

"Sorry!" Cora-Ann said, backing away. "I—I thought Jessie was in here. Really. I didn't mean to bother you."

"Hey, Cora-Ann," Josh called good-naturedly from the sofa.

"What?" Cora-Ann asked, as if she hadn't heard him. "Oh, hi." She waved.

"It's okay, Cora-Ann," Emily reassured her. She felt so relieved.

It wasn't Nancy!

"Come in," she told Cora-Ann. "You don't have to run away."

Cora-Ann blushed. "Oh, no. You know. Maybe some other time. Sorry again about. . . ." She backed down the hallway till she bumped into the wall.

Then she was gone.

Josh motioned for Emily to come back to the couch.

But the thought of Nancy at the door—even though it had turned out not to be Nancy at all—had spoiled the mood for Emily.

She slumped down on the sofa next to Josh. "Poor Cora-Ann," she said. "I feel so sorry for her. She's really a sad case."

"Emily, you feel sorry for half the people you meet."

"Well, half the people I meet are sad."

Josh rolled his eyes.

"I'm serious. Cora-Ann has it really rough. Her parents fight all the time. These past few weeks Cora-Ann has been over here so much it's like she's moved in. She's desperate to get away from her parents. Now isn't that sad? And don't roll your eyes again."

She lay back, letting his strong arms fold around her. She snuggled against his cheek. "I really like Cora-Ann—" she started.

"That's a relief," he interrupted.

"Stop. I was going to say, I really like her, but—she's always trying so hard. She can never just relax and be natural."

"Next Saturday night," he said. "You busy?"

"You're not listening to me," Emily scolded. "Let's see. Next Saturday night. I think I have to go out with one of my other boyfriends next Saturday night."

"Want to go to Red Heat?"

"Red Heat? And spend the night dancing with you? No way."

"It's a date," he declared.

Emily walked him to the door. It took him a while to leave. Which suited Emily just fine.

When Emily finally went upstairs to her room, she found Jessie sitting at the computer. "I don't believe it!" Emily cried. "Jessie Wallner starts her homework at five in the afternoon? Now I've seen everything."

Jessie pulled the chair back from the computer so that Emily could see the monitor. She was playing *Tetris*.

"All right!" Emily exclaimed. "That's more like it."

Emily picked up her empty perfume bottle from the dresser. The glass still smelled of flowers and peaches. She inhaled deeply.

"Give me a break," Jessie muttered.

Emily turned. "Excuse me?"

"The way you moon around after Josh comes over, it's sickening." Jessie eyed her closely. "Do you know how lucky you are?"

Emily couldn't help grinning. "I know."

"Hey, are you sure you're not tired of Josh?" Jessie asked, as if the thought had just occurred to her. "You know. Maybe you need a little change of pace. Want to try a new guy? And send me your discards."

"Very funny," Emily replied, rolling her eyes. She never liked it when Jessie joked about Josh this way. She got the feeling Jessie wasn't kidding.

Jessie's jealousy is really starting to make me feel uncomfortable, Emily realized.

"Want to work on our French homework together?" Emily asked, hoping to change the subject.

Jessie stood, stretched, and yawned. "No, thanks. I need something to eat."

After Jessie went downstairs, Emily lay on her bed. Glad to be alone. She closed her eyes, thinking about Josh. Then she forced herself to start her French homework.

When she finished French, she moved on to calculus, which she liked a whole lot more.

The next time she checked her bedside clock, an hour had gone by. Her shoulder felt cramped, from the way she'd been lying. Her throat felt dry.

"Thirsty," she murmured out loud.

She headed into the hall. The door to Nancy's room stood open. She stuck her head in. "Want something to drink?" she asked.

The room was empty. She found herself staring at that white sheet on the wall. She glanced behind her. She felt tempted.

No way. What am I thinking of? she scolded herself. Spying on Nancy would be a great way to make her feel comfortable being home.

Emily headed for the stairs. She reached the top landing and stopped short.

Nancy stood at the bottom of the stairs, her foot on the first step.

"Hi," Nancy called up.

"Hi."

They both started walking toward each other, one sister walking up, one walking down.

Nancy held her paintbrushes, their bristles dark and wet as if they'd been freshly cleaned. She stopped a few steps below Emily.

"You didn't go in my room, did you?" she demanded.

"In your room? No. I mean, I stuck my head in, but—"

"You looked at my mural?"

"No way," Emily replied sharply.

Wow. Was she glad she hadn't peeked at the mural! She was a terrible liar. Nancy would have known right away.

"I'm sorry," Nancy said. "I sound all paranoid, right?"

"No. No way," Emily replied quickly. She didn't sound paranoid. She had come close to the truth.

"It's just—I really don't want anyone to see it until it's done," Nancy explained.

"Okay," Emily agreed. "No problem." Why do I feel so awkward? Emily wondered. Why is there so much tension between us all of a sudden?

Nancy started up the stairs again.

"Have fun," Emily said, squeezing past her sister.

Emily had her gaze on the stairs. So she was staring straight down at Nancy's foot as—

Nancy stuck her foot out.

It was like a dream, where you're in an accident.

You're falling . . . falling. You see yourself fall, and there's nothing you can do.

No time to scream.

No time to grab the banister.

Nancy's foot had shot out.

Emily tripped over it—and went sailing headfirst down the stairs.

chapter

9

An Accident

*E*mily's shoulder slammed into the wall. Her hand scraped against the iron banister.

She hit the wooden stairs hard on her elbows and knees.

Pain shot through her body.

She tumbled once. Hit again.

This hit knocked her breath out.

Everything went black. Then very white.

Did she black out for a moment? For *more* than a moment?

She had no idea.

When she opened her eyes, squinting through the pain that throbbed behind her head, Nancy leaned over her. "Emily. Emily. Emily." Nancy repeated her name like a chant.

"You—you—" Emily shut her eyes again. Struggled to form words. Struggled to rise up from the blanketing pain.

"Emily—should I call an ambulance? Can you hear me? Are you okay?"

She felt her sister's hands on her shoulders. Gentle but firm, pulling her up. Up from the white pain.

"You—tried to *kill* me!" Emily shrieked in a hoarse voice she didn't recognize.

"Huh?" Nancy gasped. Her pale face twisted in shock.

Emily sat up with a groan. Realized she had fallen all the way down. She rubbed the throbbing ache at the back of her skull. "You tripped me. You deliberately tripped me!"

"No!" Nancy uttered a horrified cry. She jumped to her feet, green eyes wild. "No! Don't, Emily. Don't say that!"

"I saw you!" Emily insisted. "I saw your foot—"

"I didn't trip you!" Nancy shrieked. "It was an accident, Em. A horrible accident."

Emily groaned. Tried to rub away the pain. Her right arm throbbed. Both of her knees ached.

She shook her head, as if trying to shake the pain away.

"I saw your foot, Nancy. It wasn't an accident."

Nancy dropped back to her knees beside her. "You don't understand. It's the pills. The pills I have to take. They relax my muscles. They turn me into a total klutz."

"Huh?" Emily squinted at her sister, studying her face, searching for the truth.

"I'm very clumsy. My muscles don't work right.

Because of the pills." She let out a sob. "I know it was my fault, Em. But it wasn't deliberate. It was an accident. An accident."

Emily groaned in reply. Her heart slowed to normal. She started to feel a little better.

Maybe it was an accident. . . .

"Should I call an ambulance?" Nancy sobbed. "Emily? I'm going to call an ambulance!"

Emily turned her head slowly left, then right. "No. Don't. I'm—"

She moved an arm. The other one. Nothing broken. Amazing.

But she felt like one giant bruise. She glanced up the long flight of stairs. Hard to believe she had fallen most of the way down.

"Come on, Em," Nancy said tenderly, reaching for her again. "Let's get you up on your feet."

"Okay." Emily's voice came out in a whisper.

Gently, carefully, Nancy helped her to her feet. Emily stood for a moment, then slowly doubled over, hands on knees, head down, resting. Several moments later Emily took a few shaky steps around the hallway. She felt a surge of relief. She was okay.

"You sure I shouldn't call a doctor or someone?" Nancy asked.

"Positive," Emily answered curtly.

Emily felt confused. Did she have a right to be angry or didn't she?

"How do you feel now?" Nancy anxiously searched her face.

"Better. A lot better."

But her mind spun, as if she were still falling down the stairs.

Was my fall really an accident? she wondered.

Was it?

chapter
10

Everyone Hates Emily

*T*he white-uniformed cafeteria worker held her metal ladle in the air, waiting for Emily's decision.

"I guess I'll take a sloppy joe," Emily said.

The woman scooped up meat and sauce and poured it over an open bun. She passed the plate across the glass counter.

Smells pretty good, Emily thought. Most kids brought their lunch, but Emily liked something hot.

She carried her tray through the noisy cafeteria, searching for Josh. She didn't find him. Then she scanned the crowded room for Jessie. No sign of her, either.

But at the far end of the dining hall, her head down over her tray, wasn't that—?

Cora-Ann.

Emily made her way across the room toward her.

"Where's Jessie?" she asked as she sat down across from her.

Cora-Ann stared at her blankly for a moment. Then she smiled. "Oh, hey. I don't know, I didn't see her. Probably hiding from me." She grinned. "I hang around her too much."

"That's not what she says," Emily replied.

Poor Cora-Ann. She looked unhappy. Her eyes were rimmed with red. "You okay?" Emily asked.

"Me? Oh, yeah, sure." Cora-Ann sighed. "How about you?"

Emily didn't answer. Just stared at Cora-Ann.

Cora-Ann didn't hold out for long. "I don't look so hot, right? I know. It's nothing. It's just . . ." She rubbed her face. "Home. You know."

"Tell me about it," Emily agreed. "Rich is planning to kill me. And I think Nancy pushed me down the front stairs. It's getting so I only feel safe at school."

She took a bite of her sandwich. Waited for Cora-Ann to reply. "Are you listening? Or did you go someplace far away?"

Cora-Ann covered her face with both hands, then pulled them away. "I'm sorry," she replied. "It's just . . . I know your family is messed up. But at least you *have* a family. My dad moved out last week."

Last week? Jessie hadn't said a word.

"Wow," Emily muttered. "I'm sorry."

Cora-Ann sighed again. "I haven't told anyone, not even Jessie. I just keep hoping he'll come back, you know."

I know, thought Emily. She still hoped her father would come back—and he was dead.

"That's rough," Emily told her. "I'm sorry."

"You don't know," Cora-Ann blurted out with emotion. "My mom is so upset. And I can understand that. Hey, I'm upset, too, you know? But it's like Mom doesn't even know I'm alive. I'm totally alone with this. I'm fifteen, and I'm already on my own!"

"Well," Emily said gently, "you have us, Cora-Ann."

She couldn't help feeling guilty. Lots of times Emily had wished Cora-Ann didn't hang around the Wallner house so much. She had even told Jessie so a couple of times. She hoped that Jessie had never passed along the message to Cora-Ann.

"Milk bomb!" someone yelled.

"Incoming!" cried a second voice.

A milk carton sailed over Emily's head. The carton splattered against the lunchroom wall. Emily heard cheers. And angry shouts.

"Very mature," Emily commented. "Can you believe some of these kids will be going to college next year?"

Emily raised her eyes and saw Jessie, across the lunchroom, a food tray in her hands.

Emily waved.

Jessie stared back—then turned away as if she hadn't seen her.

Weird, Emily thought. Is Jessie angry at me about something?

I hope not. I don't think I could handle anyone else hating me now. Try me again in a week.

Emily's first class after lunch was chem lab. With everything that had been going on, Emily had a little trouble concentrating. Her lab partner became very impatient, especially after Emily broke her second beaker.

Finally the bell rang. Emily joined the crowd of students hurrying out of the lab.

She gasped as Jessie popped out in front of her.

"What were you and Cora-Ann talking about?" Jessie demanded, arms crossed.

"Oh, Jessie. You scared me. I thought you saw me waving! Why didn't you come over?"

The hallway had quickly filled with noisy students, everyone yelling, banging locker doors, getting books for the next period. Emily could hardly hear.

Jessie grabbed her arm. "I said, what were the two of you talking about? Every time I looked over, it was like you were having the world's most serious discussion."

"We were talking about her family," Emily replied. "Her dad left." She felt strange talking about Cora-Ann's personal problems so loudly, but it was the only way to be heard.

The second bell rang, piercing through the noise. The hallway began to empty out. "Her dad left?" Jessie asked, surprised. "She never said a word to me."

"I know," Emily replied. "That's Cora-Ann. She's

66

trying to win the Nobel Prize for niceness. She told me she didn't want to bother us with her problems."

"Yeah. But why did she tell *you* instead of *me?*" Jessie demanded, sounding hurt.

Emily shrugged. "You weren't there."

Jessie glared at her a moment, then backed away, headed for her locker. She pointed an accusing finger at Emily. "She's *my* friend, Emily. Don't forget it!"

Emily watched Jessie turn down the hallway. Wow, she thought. Jessie really *is* jealous of me.

Does she hate me, too?

Jessie. Nancy. Rich. Is my whole family against me?

chapter

11

A Nasty Cut

*E*mily had always hated the basement in her house. Too many cobwebs, too many dusty corners. She seldom ventured down here. But early Saturday evening Jessie and Cora-Ann insisted she join them downstairs to play Ping-Pong.

They all became bored with the game pretty quickly. Jessie stood banging Ping-Pong balls into the far recesses of the dark basement for Butch to fetch.

"Don't feel bad, Emily," Jessie told her glumly. She whacked another ball. This time Butch didn't bother going after it. "Just because you have a date tonight, and Cora-Ann and I are stuck at home." *Whack.*

Cora-Ann twirled her paddle on the table. "Hey, don't get so down," she told Jessie. "One Saturday night we don't have dates. Big deal."

Jessie arched a blond eyebrow. *"One* Saturday night?"

"Okay. Two in a row," Cora-Ann admitted.

Emily could hardly believe Jessie had such bad luck with guys. With Jessie's looks, Emily thought, the guys should be knocking the door down. But they weren't even calling.

She knelt down and examined a jigsaw puzzle that had been left on the floor, half done—a picture of a windmill in Holland.

She tried to fit a tulip piece into the foreground. "Who's doing this puzzle? Jessie? Are you?"

"Not me," Jessie answered.

"Not me," Cora-Ann added.

"Must be Nancy," Jessie volunteered.

Emily gazed up at the ceiling, as if Nancy might be staring down at her from the shadows. Nancy spent most of her time alone in her room these days. That was bad enough. The thought of her sister alone in the basement doing jigsaw puzzles made Emily want to cry.

"How's Nancy doing?" Cora-Ann asked in a whisper.

She must have caught Emily's mood. Ever since Nancy had returned from the hospital, Emily couldn't shake the feeling that her sister was eavesdropping, spying on her, listening in.

Emily shrugged. "Okay, I guess. But she's cooped up in the house all day. I mean, it's not like she's got a lot of friends. She certainly doesn't have any dates."

"Tell me about it," Jessie said bitterly.

The basement door creaked open. They all froze.

"Hello?" Nancy called. "Anyone down there?"

"Hey!" Emily called.

Nancy came down a few steps, then peered over the banister.

"There you are," she said. She held a small cardboard box. "Guess what I found at the back of my closet?"

She shook the box. It rattled. "Scrabble!" she announced.

Emily groaned. Nancy, she knew, was the world's best Scrabble player. She practically knew every word in the dictionary. She and Emily had had to stop playing Scrabble long ago—because Nancy always won so easily.

"You guys want to play?" Nancy asked.

"Emily can't," Jessie answered. "She's got a date with Josh."

Nancy frowned. "Oh. That's right. But what about—"

"I'd love to play," Cora-Ann said.

Cora-Ann and Emily both stared at Jessie. Cornered, Jessie shrugged and said, "I'll play. But I stink at it. I can't spell."

"All right!" Nancy cried. She came down the stairs, shaking the box over her head. "We're going to play Scrabble!" She did a little dance, laughing.

Poor Nancy, thought Emily. She couldn't believe anyone could get that excited over a game.

"Hey, if that makes you happy," Jessie said, "we've got a great evening planned for you. Cora-Ann rented two movies."

Nancy clutched the Scrabble box with both hands.

"Oh, I'm so glad to be home!" she cried suddenly. She twirled slowly in a circle on the dark basement floor.

"Because we're playing Scrabble?" Jessie asked.

"Believe me," Nancy told her. "After the year I've had, a movie and a game of Scrabble are an exciting evening!"

Emily hadn't thought about that in a while—what Nancy's year must have been like. At least Nancy is happy now, she thought.

Nancy shoved the magazines off the old coffee table, then wiped away the dust with her bare hand. She opened the Scrabble box and dumped out the wooden tiles.

"I don't really remember how to play," Cora-Ann said as she peered at the pile of letter blocks.

"Don't worry, I'll teach you," Nancy told her.

Emily pushed herself to her feet. "Well, I should get ready, I guess." She hated to remind the three girls she was going off on her date. She felt as if she were betraying them somehow.

"See you," Nancy called, without looking up. "Now first we turn all the tiles facedown," she told Jessie and Cora-Ann. She started nimbly flicking over the tiny wooden tiles.

"Are we allowed to make up words?" Jessie asked as Emily headed up the stairs.

She had only about ten minutes to get ready. That was okay. She knew exactly what she wanted to wear to the dance club.

The black dress. Her favorite. It was so short and sexy.

71

She started up the carpeted front steps.

Jessie had borrowed the dress several times, including three weeks ago when she and Cora-Ann went off dancing by themselves, hoping to meet guys. Jessie looked absolutely fabulous in the dress, of course.

But Emily couldn't worry about that. It was still her dress. And it was still her Josh.

She opened the door to her room. The dry cleaner bag hung right where she left it, on the inside of the closet door. The last time Jessie wore the dress, she had left a food stain on it. But the cleaners had promised Emily it would come out without a problem.

She lifted the bag and held it against her body. The cellophane crinkled. She loved the way the cleaners wrapped clothes in cellophane. It made her feel as if her clothes were some big present for her to open.

She pulled the cellophane up and over the wooden hanger.

"No!" she choked out. "Oh, nooo."

The dress had been sliced down the middle.

chapter

12

Snip, Snip

Emily didn't even realize she was shouting until Jessie, Cora-Ann, and Nancy all burst into the room.

"What? What happened?" Jessie cried.

"We heard you—all the way from the basement," Cora-Ann gasped. "Are you okay?"

Nancy is the only one who isn't asking what happened, Emily realized.

Why isn't Nancy asking?

Because she already knows.

Silently Emily held out the dress. She didn't trust herself to say a word. If she opened her mouth, she'd start shouting again. Or crying.

Cora-Ann let out a long breath. She came forward and gently took the ruined dress in her hands. "You know what?" she said, examining it carefully. "The pressing machine must have done it."

"The *what?*" Emily demanded.

"The pressing machine. The same thing happened to my best blouse once. The cleaners run everything through these big machines, and sometimes—"

"You think this was an accident?" Emily cried, her voice rising.

Cora-Ann gave her a worried stare. "Well, I—"

"It was no accident!" Emily shrieked.

"Can I see?" Nancy asked. She stepped forward and started to study the dress.

Emily pulled it away from her. "You've already seen it," she said, her voice trembling.

Nancy reacted with surprise. "Huh? No, I was thinking maybe I could sew it," she said. She gave Emily another quick glance, then turned back to the dress. "But I don't think . . ." Her voice trailed off.

Nancy and her dirty tricks, Emily thought bitterly.

Maybe Nancy had tricked the doctors, too, tricked them into letting her come home before she was really cured. She stared at Nancy coldly.

Nancy met her gaze. Her eyes widened. "You think *I* did this?" she asked, her voice trembling.

Nancy sounded so hurt.

Emily wanted to say no. She wanted to tell Nancy that she trusted her. But she couldn't get the words out. "Did you do it?" she asked softly.

"Why?" Nancy asked, biting her lip. "Why would I want to ruin your dress? Tell me that!"

"She's not saying you did," Cora-Ann chimed in, placing a hand on Nancy's arm.

Nancy pulled her arm free. "Yes, she is! She's accusing me, as she always does."

"I'm not saying a word," Emily insisted.

Nancy shook her head bitterly. "Whenever anything goes wrong, you just assume—"

Her voice broke. With a sob, she turned and ran from the room. A moment later her door slammed.

"Em—" Jessie began.

Emily didn't wait to hear the rest. She rushed out of the room. Down the hall to Nancy's room. She couldn't stand the thought of Nancy being so upset, even if she *had* cut the dress.

She knocked.

No answer.

"Nancy, please!" she called in. "I didn't say you cut the dress. Honestly. I didn't even think it," she lied.

She could hear Nancy moving around in the room. Then silence. She tried the doorknob.

Locked.

She stood at the door for a moment more, begging her sister to let her in.

Then she gave up.

At the end of the hall the door to Rich's room stood open for once. Emily took a few steps toward his room.

She found Rich sitting on the floor, cutting a piece of blue construction paper with a large pair of scissors.

Light glinted off the long, sharp blades.

He raised his head, meeting her gaze.

He grinned at her.

Then he lifted up the scissors.

"Snip, snip," he said.

chapter

13

"I Will Trust Nancy"

"Snip, snip," Emily told her mother the next day. "He raised the scissors like this, and he went 'Snip, snip.'"

"That's it?" Mrs. Wallner stopped scrubbing the already spotless stove and frowned at Emily. "He didn't say anything else?"

"Like what?"

"I don't know. He didn't make any specific threats?"

"He said he was going to stab me sixteen times. Okay? You satisfied?" Emily snapped.

"Emily!" Mrs. Wallner gasped. "How can you joke about something like this?"

Emily didn't reply.

What a Sunday, she thought miserably.

While her mother cleaned, Emily sat at the kitchen table in her big house smock. The Sunday newspaper crossword puzzle lay open on the table in front of her.

She hadn't gotten too far. She had filled in 29 down and 103 across. So far that was it.

Mrs. Wallner sighed. "Hugh and I are so worried about Rich, I can't tell you. There's no doubt about it. He's a very troubled boy. We're trying to find a therapist he can talk to. But—"

There was always a *but.*

"But in the meantime . . . I don't know. Just try to stay on his good side, okay? You know, go easy on him. Can you do that?" Mrs. Wallner asked.

"Yeah, don't worry," Emily replied. "It'll be okay."

Why did she always end up having to reassure her mother? Shouldn't her mother reassure her?

She heard shouts from outside. She stared out the little window over the sink. It had snowed a little last night, dusting the trees and bushes, like a topping of powdered sugar. Emily could see Cora-Ann and Jessie trying to build a snowman out of the powdery snow.

"How are you and Nancy getting along?" her mother asked. She made it sound like a casual question. As if she hadn't been up all night worrying about the answer.

"Okay," Emily said.

"Just okay?" Mrs. Wallner studied her face.

"I'm still frightened of her, I guess," Emily admitted.

"Afraid? Of Nancy?" Mrs. Wallner pointed out the window with her soapy Brillo pad. "Look at her, Emily. She's so happy to be home. She's totally changed. That's one thing I can promise you. You have no reason to be afraid of Nancy."

Emily gazed out the window. She watched Nancy wandering around the yard, huddled in her red coat. She felt a terrible wrench of pity. Why didn't Nancy go hang out with Jessie and Cora-Ann? And why didn't they try to include her?

"Emily."

She turned. Her mother had that overly serious and hurt expression on her face. It was an expression that Emily had never been able to resist.

"What?"

"Remember that talk we had? The day Nancy came home? When you promised me—"

"I know." Please stop staring at me like that, she silently begged.

"I'm counting on you, Emily. I'm counting on you to help her come back to her herself. Nancy—she's always loved you the most, you know."

The lump. It was back in Emily's throat. Instantly.

"That's not true," she managed to say.

Loved me the most? Is that why she tried to kill me?

"If I know Nancy," her mother continued, "and I think I do, she'll never, ever be able to forgive herself for what she almost did to you."

Almost? thought Emily. There were plenty of horrible things Nancy had done to her, no *almost* about it.

"But if you would forgive her," continued Mrs. Wallner, her voice breaking, "I just think . . ."

"Oh, right," said Emily. "So it's up to me."

Her mother turned away.

Emily stared out the window. Nancy had disappeared. She waited. Finally Nancy reappeared. She

78

was coming out of the garage, carrying their stepfather's tool kit.

That's odd, thought Emily.

She felt the old suspicions rising inside her. Nancy is right, she thought. No matter what she does, I'll always be suspicious of her. Always.

She stood up from the table. "I already told Nancy that I forgive her, Mom. She doesn't believe me."

Mrs. Wallner nodded. "That's because she's very sensitive. She won't believe you until you really mean it, Em."

Emily slipped her hands into the deep front pockets of the smock. She rocked back and forth on her bare heels. She was trying not to think about what her mother had just said.

Her mother had a way of making comments that worked their way into your ears and all the way down to your toes. Was she right? Had Emily really forgiven Nancy?

Emily was still wrestling with that question ten minutes later. She'd pulled on some warm clothes and taken Butch outside for his walk. Butch started running around like crazy, sniffing everywhere, trying to find his scent and markings under the snow.

When Butch saw Jessie and Cora-Ann, he raced off, his little ears flapping. The two girls had succeeded in building a little snowman. They waved to Emily to come over. She waved back. She wanted to find Nancy.

Emily saw Nancy step out of the woods that bordered the backyard. Her cheeks were red. She had pulled her hood back, and her red hair shone in the bright sun. Circles of red marked her cheeks like a Santa Claus. She was grinning and swinging the tool kit from side to side.

It was like a vision. A vision from the past. The old Nancy.

Emily hurried out to meet her, suddenly feeling excited.

"Hey!" Nancy said.

"Hey," Emily said back.

They grinned at each other. Nancy turned and swung the tool kit back toward the woods. "I fixed the tree house. The missing rung."

"You did? That's great!"

Nancy's face filled with surprise. "What are you so excited about?"

"Just in a good mood, I guess."

Nancy laughed and rubbed the top of Emily's head. "You jerk."

Emily grabbed Nancy's hand and they sort of wrestled, sort of hugged.

"Hey, I thought you were going to see Josh," Nancy said, wiping her nose with the back of her hand.

"Soon," Emily said.

"Well, tell him I said hi."

Emily searched Nancy's face for sarcasm, but found none.

Mom is right, thought Emily. Nancy seems so much more relaxed. Nancy appeared so happy, Emily could almost make herself believe that none of the horror had ever happened.

And right then, Emily made a silent vow:

I will trust Nancy! I won't accuse her anymore. Not out loud or even in my thoughts.

Nancy stood watching Jessie and Cora-Ann work on their snowman.

"Yo, Wallner!" Nancy called to Jessie. "That is one pitiful snowman."

Jessie gazed up, surprised. So did Cora-Ann. Even Butch turned.

"Think you and Emily can do better?" Jessie taunted.

"In our sleep," Nancy replied. She and Emily started walking toward the other two girls, their boots crunching on the thin layer of snow.

"That's no snowman," Emily teased as they came closer. "That's a snowworm."

"The snow is too thin," Cora-Ann complained. She scooped up a mittenful of white powder to show them.

"Let's see if it sticks," Emily said. She started making a snowball.

"Watch out, Cora-Ann!" cried Jessie, her blue eyes sparkling.

Emily tossed the powdery ball at Cora-Ann. It broke into a shower of cold dust.

Jessie grabbed the snow shovel. She pushed it along the yard, scooping up a large pile of snow. Then she heaved it all at Nancy.

Nancy shrieked happily. Emily tackled Jessie from behind. They rolled over and over in the snow, shouting, snow clinging to their hair.

Butch barked madly, adding his own cries to the shouts and laughter. They stopped trying to throw the snow at one another. They started tossing it up in the air instead, watching it sparkle as it showered down on them.

Mrs. Wallner's amazed face appeared at the small kitchen window.

Everyone screamed and jumped and waved. Giggling wildly, they all flopped down on the ground and started making snow angels.

What an amazing feeling, thought Emily.

We are actually having fun.

Emily didn't leave for Josh's house until six. The snowball fight had put her in such a great mood. She was humming as she headed out to the garage.

A dark, starless night. Emily shivered, watching her breath stream out in front of her.

It wasn't until she came around the corner that she remembered the garage light. She had turned the light on from the house. She had forgotten that the bulb was burned out.

The garage hulked in the darkness. Emily groped for the icy metal handle of the garage door and yanked upward. The door rattled and rumbled, metal scraping against metal.

If she had to choose among the basement, the attic, and the garage for scariest place in the Wallner house, the garage would win hands down. Opening the door was like opening the door to a giant coffin.

Her eyes adjusted to the darkness inside the garage. Strange dark shapes lined the garage walls.

Shovels, sleds, she told herself. Nothing scary.

Why was she convinced that something was about to jump out at her?

She fumbled with the key, trying to fit it into the lock in the car door.

Finally she pulled the door open. The car light came on.

Emily slid behind the wheel. The leather seats felt cold and hard.

She backed the car down the icy drive.

Then she stepped on the gas, eager to get to Josh's house.

The icy road twisted past the Fear Street woods. The car skidded as she followed the curve.

She gripped the wheel.

Glancing down, she checked the speedometer. Fifty mph. She really should slow down, she scolded herself. The speed limit on this stretch of the road was thirty-five, and that was the limit during good weather.

She pressed down on the brake pedal gently.

But the car didn't slow down at all.

She pressed the brake harder.

The car raced ahead.

Emily swallowed hard, gripping the wheel tightly.

This isn't happening to me, she thought, frozen in dread.

No. Please—!

She held her breath. Floored the brake pedal.

Floored it. Released. Floored it. Released. Stomped on it. Again and again.

The car raced forward.

No brakes, Emily realized. No brakes.

I'm going to die.

chapter
14

Car Repair

No brakes. No brakes.

Emily let out a shriek of panic as the car whipped around the next turn.

She spun the wheel wildly, struggling to keep control.

But the car skidded sideways over an icy patch of road.

No brakes. No brakes!

The blast of an air horn drowned out her scream.

The windshield filled with an icy white light. Headlights of a truck.

She twisted the wheel as the truck screamed toward her.

Too late!

No brakes! *No brakes!*

She felt a blast of air as the truck roared past.

Missed by inches!

But the car skidded off the road. Up a hill. Onto a lawn.

"Nooooooo!"

Emily saw the dark tree trunk in the glare of her headlights.

Her head snapped back. She saw the trunk in her windshield. Heard the crunch of metal. The shatter of glass.

No brakes! No brakes!

Her last thought before everything went silver-white. Then black.

". . . results were negative, Mister Wallner . . ."

A woman's voice. A man's. The woman's again.

Other faint sounds. Padded footsteps. Metal wheels squeaking against waxed floors.

Hard to hear over the pounding in her skull.

Emily opened her eyes. She focused on a white tileboard ceiling. She turned. Moving was hard, painful.

She lay on her back in a bed. When she turned her head to the side, she saw thick aluminum bars lining her bed like a mini-prison. Beyond the bars stood a plastic bag on a metal stand.

An IV bag?

She was in the hospital.

She followed the snaky white plastic line from the IV line down, down, down. She was terrified that the IV line led to her arm.

It didn't. It led to the floor. The IV bag wasn't connected to her.

Emily sat up with a groan.

She was alone in a tiny hospital room the size of a large closet. The door stood open. Outside in the hall she could see a pair of legs, familiar brown corduroy slacks—Mr. Wallner. Talking to someone in a white lab coat.

"The E.E.G. was also normal, Mr. Wallner."

She heard her stepfather sigh with relief. "That is wonderful news. Thank you, Doctor."

Are they talking about me? Emily wondered groggily.

The tree slammed full force into her memory. The big, dark trunk attacked the windshield.

Her next thought made Emily lurch forward in horror.

Nancy.

Nancy carrying the tool kit.

Nancy fiddled with the brakes!

"Hey, she's up!" Mr. Wallner cried, hurrying into the room.

"Dad, there's something we have to talk about," Emily said through gritted teeth.

"Dr. Sorenson said you're perfectly okay! How about that?" He winked.

"I said I have to talk to you, Dad. *Please.*"

"They said you can come home, Em, if you feel up to it."

"Now, Dad!" Emily cried.

Mr. Wallner sat down in the red vinyl chair near the head of the bed. He ran his hands tensely over his bald head. He stared at her, waiting. "What? What's wrong?"

"Is my sister here?" Emily asked softly, as if Nancy might be at the door, listening.

"Jessie?" asked Mr. Wallner.

"No! Nancy."

"Oh. No. Nobody else is here, Em. Your mom took the girls to a movie right after you left, so I was the only one home when the hospital called. I left them a note. Told them you had an accident." He shook his head at the memory. "Wow. Was *that* a scary phone call!"

"Dad—" she began.

But then, she felt unsure. Should she tell him her suspicions? He and Mom were both so unwilling to believe anything bad about Nancy.

And Emily had been wrong about Nancy before.

Or had she?

Stalling for time, she asked, "How's the car?"

Mr. Wallner shook his head. "Is that what you're worried about? I'm afraid I don't have good news on that front. According to the police, the car is totaled." He sighed. "The cop told me that when we see the car, we're not going to believe you survived the . . . the, um . . ." His voice caught.

His eyes watered over.

Emily stared at him in shock. She never realized her stepfather cared about her that much.

"Well," Mr. Wallner said, rising. "I guess we should—"

"Nancy did it," Emily blurted out.

Mr. Wallner's mouth dropped open. "What are you talking about? Nancy did what?"

"Nancy tried to kill me. She messed with the brakes. Loosened them. Or cut them. Or whatever you do to brakes. She did it."

"Emily—" Mr. Wallner tightened his hands into fists. He searched for the right words. "You know how your mother and I feel about accusing Nancy of things just because—"

"I saw her coming out of the garage with your tool kit. Then she said she wanted to fix the tree house. My sister tried to kill me. She won't stop until I'm dead. You've got to do something. You've got to—"

He put a hand on her arm, pushing her gently back against the pillows. He looked toward the open door, as if he were hoping a nurse would come.

"Emily," he said quietly, "it's not Nancy's fault. It's mine."

He stared at her, his eyes locked on hers, waiting for her reaction. Emily's jaw dropped. Her stepfather? Mr. Wallner tried to kill her? "You?! You loosened the brakes?"

"What? Oh, no. What I mean is, the accident. I blame myself. For weeks I've been thinking those brakes were a little loose. I've been telling myself I should bring the car in to the shop. But I was so worried about Nancy coming home, and the factory—I just never got around to having them fixed."

"Dad, stop it!" Emily cried so angrily that Mr. Wallner's head jerked back in surprise. "Don't cover for her! Nancy did this. I know it!"

Mr. Wallner shook his head. "That doesn't make sense, Em. Even if she wanted to, how would Nancy know how to ruin the brakes on a car?"

Emily felt a chill. "Car repair," she murmured.

"Excuse me?"

"Nancy said she studied car repair. At the hospital."

"Emily," Mr. Wallner said softly, "you're beginning to worry me. Maybe that knock on the head did some real damage after all."

Unbelievable, thought Emily. They just won't listen. What will it take?

"Come on," Mr. Wallner said gently, "let's get you home."

As he helped her out of the bed, she said, "Do me a favor. When Nancy finally succeeds in killing me, ground her for a few weeks, okay?"

"Emily—" Mr. Wallner started. He looked so hurt that Emily wished she had never said it.

The house was dark when they got home. Mr. Wallner held on to her firmly as he guided her up the icy walk.

As they came in the front door, Rich came out of the kitchen carrying a carton of ice cream. Rich was spooning the ice cream directly out of the carton.

"That belongs in a dish, Mister," Mr. Wallner snapped at him. "How many times do I have to tell you these things?"

Rich did a U-turn back into the kitchen.

Mr. Wallner yelled after him. "Aren't you even going to ask Emily how she is? She just had a very serious car accident, you know."

Rich stuck his head back out of the kitchen doorway. "I hope you're okay," he told Emily.

He didn't even try to sound sincere.

Someone was crying.

Sad, muffled sobs.

I'm dreaming, Emily told herself. I'm dreaming that someone is crying. Don't wake up. Need my sleep.

The next cry was longer and harder. It woke her up for real.

She opened her eyes and stared into darkness.

Where am I? she wondered. The hospital? Home?

Her mind cleared. It was Tuesday night. Two nights since she had slammed the car into a tree.

She was home. She was safe.

Another sob interrupted her thoughts.

"Jessie?" she whispered.

She rolled over, turning toward the sound of the crying.

"Jessie? What is it? What's wrong?"

chapter

15

More Nightmares

*E*mily fumbled for the light on her nightstand.

Jessie was sitting up in bed, one hand covering her face. "Turn that off," she ordered. Adding a pitiful, "Please."

Emily clicked off the light.

"What's wrong?" Emily repeated.

"Nothing. I just . . . feel so guilty!"

"Guilty about what?" Emily whispered.

"About Jolie," Jessie said, crying some more.

Emily clicked the light back on. This time Jessie didn't object.

"Another nightmare about Jolie?"

Jessie nodded. "That day she died on the camping trip . . . I was thinking, Jolie, I hope you die! I was thinking those exact words."

"Jessie—"

"What?"

"Thinking mean things about someone is totally normal. Everyone does that. You didn't have anything to do with her accident. You can't blame yourself, just because you had bad thoughts."

Jessie blew her nose. "Thanks, Em," she said.

"You know," Emily continued, "sometimes I feel guilty, too. Like maybe I could have saved my father before he drowned. But I know that isn't true. You and I, Jessie. We have to start giving ourselves a break."

Jessie looked up at Emily, tears glistening on her pale cheeks. "You're—you're a great sister," she stammered.

"You, too," Emily replied softly. "You—you had the same nightmare?"

Jessie nodded. She had told Emily about her bad dreams enough times that Emily could picture every scene. Jolie going over the cliff in slow motion, arms thrashing through the air. Jessie surrounded in the dark woods. And then the strange dark figures starting to come at her from all sides.

Emily shuddered. "Do you think nightmares are contagious?"

"Huh? What do you mean?"

"I don't know. With my luck, I'll start dreaming your bad dreams along with mine."

Jessie lowered her gaze. "I'm sorry I woke you up. I tried to be quiet, but I was just feeling so low. I mean, I can't believe I'm having these bad dreams again."

Jessie gave her a worried look. "You don't mind me saying that, do you?"

"Just relax—" Emily started.

"I was just lying here feeling as if this will never go away," Jessie said. "I thought, this nightmare will never stop. My whole life. You know?"

"Believe me, I do."

"Right, you know better than anyone. And then—I just started remembering all this stuff about Jolie. We were so close. Until all the bad stuff happened between us. When we were fighting over this guy."

She was silent for a moment. Then she climbed to her feet, crossed the room, and opened the top drawer of the dresser. She reached deep inside and pulled out a cigar box that Emily had never seen before.

"You're not going to smoke in here or something, are you?" Emily asked.

"Huh?" Jessie glanced at her, then down at the cigar box. She smiled. She pulled a rubber band off the box, then fished around inside.

"I never showed you this," Jessie said. She was holding a small Polaroid snapshot. She sat down on the bed next to Emily and studied the picture. Finally she handed it over. "Here," she said softly. "That's Jolie."

Emily took the picture by the edges. She held the small picture up close to the lamp.

Then she gasped in shock.

"What?" Jessie asked, alarmed. "What's wrong?"

"Jessie—" Emily cried. "Don't you realize who Jolie looks like?"

chapter
16

Her Lips Are Sealed

"Who?" Jessie demanded, peering over Emily's shoulder.

"Cora-Ann!" Emily exclaimed.

"She does?" Jessie took the photo back, peering at it up close. "Wow. I never noticed."

"Oh, come on," Emily said. "Look at those dark eyes, the round face."

"I guess there is a resemblance," Jessie said, still staring at the snapshot.

"A resemblance?! When I first looked at it, I thought you handed me a picture of Cora-Ann."

Jessie studied the picture a while longer. Then she turned back to Emily, puzzled. "You think Cora-Ann could be reminding me of Jolie without my even realizing it?"

"It's possible," Emily replied.

Jessie squinted at the tiny photo. "So maybe *that's* why I started dreaming about Jolie again."

* * *

Emily stared at the phone. She wanted to call Josh.

No way, she scolded herself, staring at the blue screen of her computer monitor. No phone calls until I finish this English paper.

She had written only two pages. The paper had to be at least six pages long.

Okay, she told herself, I won't call Josh until I've finished the next paragraph.

She typed one word more—*the*—then gave up and reached for the phone.

She heard voices leaking out of the receiver as she lifted it to her ear.

"Willy, I can't go," Rich was saying. "No way. I'm grounded. Remember?"

"You're still grounded?" Emily heard Willy reply. "What did your father give you? A life sentence?"

Hang up, Emily told herself. But she kept listening.

"So sneak out," Willy urged Rich.

Rich didn't answer.

"I'm telling you," Willy insisted, "Mick has a six-pack at his house. His parents won't be home till midnight at the earliest."

Emily gently placed the receiver back in its cradle, hoping Rich wouldn't hear the click.

She went back to her English paper. Mrs. Carter had assigned everyone the same topic. "What Happens to Holden Caulfield After the Book *Catcher in the Rye* Ends."

Emily actually thought the subject was interesting. But she couldn't concentrate.

Five minutes later she stared at the phone again. Rich had to be off the line by now.

She reached for the receiver—

Bang! The bedroom door flew open so hard, the doorknob chipped a chunk of plaster off the wall.

Rich burst into the doorway, glaring at her. Her hand remained frozen on the receiver.

"Don't bother listening in," he growled. "I'm already off."

"Oh, good," Emily stammered, "I was just—"

"Why do you keep spying on me?" he demanded furiously.

"Rich, I'm not. Really. I picked up the phone to make a call. I had no way of knowing that—"

"I heard you! I heard you on the line!"

"I listened for one second," Emily admitted. "But then when I realized you guys were on the phone, I—"

Rich slammed the wall with the flat of his hand. "I've had it, Emily!" he warned. "You understand?"

He was in such a fury—so out of control—Emily began to tremble.

"Just what do I have to do to you, huh?" he snarled. "You tell me. What do I have to do to you to get you to *stay out of my life?*"

Tom Hanks reached out and took Meg Ryan's hand. Emily was crying into a tissue.

If only . . . If only her life could be as simple and romantic as a movie.

The credits started to roll. Emily hit the Stop button on the VCR remote and started to rewind the tape.

"Jess . . ."

"Mmm?"

Jessie lay on her back on the leather sofa. She opened her eyes. "Oh, wow. When did I fall asleep?"

"Right before they got to the Empire State Building," Emily told her. "Which is only the most romantic part. I don't know why you always rent this movie. You always fall asleep."

Jessie sat up and rubbed her eyes. "That's why I keep renting it, I keep hoping I'll see it through to the end."

"Come on," Emily said. "We'd better get some sleep. It's after midnight."

"Okay," Jessie agreed sleepily. She yawned. "What time is it, anyway?"

Emily laughed. "I just told you. It's—"

The doorbell rang.

She and Jessie stared at each other.

"Check who it is first," Jessie warned as Emily hurried to the door.

Emily glanced through the curtains of the living room window. Then she yanked open the door.

There stood Cora-Ann, a white canvas overnight bag slung over one shoulder. "I'm sorry. I hope I didn't wake you up, but—Dad came back. And—they're fighting worse than ever."

"Worse than ever?" Jessie murmured. "Wow."

Cora-Ann swallowed hard. Her eyes were red-rimmed. She had been crying, Emily saw.

"I hate to ask this. But can I sleep over?"

She dropped the canvas bag on the floor.

Jessie wrapped her arms around her, giving Cora-Ann a long hug. "Don't worry," she murmured. "It's going to get better. Right, Emily?"

Emily forced as much enthusiasm into her "Yes!" as she could.

"Come on," Jessie told Cora-Ann, "we'd better get some sleep."

It wasn't their first unplanned slumber party. Usually, Emily liked having Cora-Ann sleeping over. But tonight for some reason, Emily couldn't fall asleep. She lay in bed, listening to Jessie and Cora-Ann, breathing slowly and deeply.

What do I have to do to you? she kept hearing Rich say.

When her alarm clock went off in the morning, Emily felt as if she had just begun to sleep.

It can't be time for school, she thought miserably. It can't. There's some mistake. She hit the snooze button.

The next time the alarm went off, she just hit Off. When she woke up again, it was ten after nine. She was late for school.

She groaned and sat up. To Emily's surprise, Jessie

99

was still in bed. Cora-Ann stood in her white night-gown, shaking Jessie. "Jess, we're late—let's go."

Jessie moaned.

Cora-Ann pulled Jessie's arm. "You use the bathroom first."

"You go," Jessie moaned. "I don't think my legs are working yet."

"No way," Cora-Ann said. "I always take the longest. Morning, Emily."

"Morning," Emily mumbled.

Cora-Ann gave Jessie another tug. "Get going, Jess."

Emily rubbed her face several times. "I'll go first," she told them.

Emily trudged into the bathroom, flicking on the light.

She stared at her face in the mirror. The pillow had mushed one side of her hair. She tugged at her hair, but the flat shape remained. Beautiful.

She spun the tap and let the water gush until it had turned ice cold. She splashed two handfuls on her face, then pressed her face into a towel.

Then she started brushing her teeth.

She kept her head down as she brushed. She didn't want to see her reflection any more than she had to.

That's odd, she thought. The toothpaste tastes so bitter—

She stopped brushing. And lowered her eyes to the toothbrush.

Uh-oh. She clenched her jaw tightly.

Her teeth stuck together.

She tried to scream. But she couldn't pry her jaws apart.

What is happening?

And then she saw the tiny green tube in the waste-basket.

The tiny green tube labeled *Super Glue*.

chapter
17

Coming Unglued

N₀! Please—no! Emily begged silently.
Super Glue in the toothpaste?

Emily grabbed the toothpaste and squeezed a ribbon of goo onto her fingers. She rubbed her fingers together.

Sure enough, her fingers stuck together. She turned on the tap as hard as it would go and lowered her head to the sink. She craned her head as she tried to direct the water over her teeth.

Her teeth still wouldn't open.

Sobbing, her heart pounding, Emily lurched out of the bathroom.

Jessie still lay in bed. Cora-Ann stood by the closet mirror, brushing her hair. She turned and stared at Emily. When she saw the look on Emily's face, she backed away.

Emily couldn't scream with her teeth shut. She

could barely talk. She burst into the room. "My teeth are glued! My teeth are glued!"

Cora-Ann stared at her in disbelief.

Emily threw her hands up in the air. She grabbed Jessie, shook her shoulders. "My teeth are glued!"

"Stop it!" Jessie snapped, shoving Emily away. "That's not funny!"

Frantically Emily turned toward the open doorway. Nancy.

Nancy did this to me.

She clenched her teeth even tighter, struggling to control her rage.

She had an idea. She plunged back into the bathroom. She dropped to her knees and dumped the contents of the wastebasket onto the floor. She grabbed the small green tube and tried to read the warning label on the back.

But tears covered her eyes. She couldn't make out the tiny white letters.

Cora-Ann stuck her head into the bathroom.

"Read this!" Emily barked through her clenched teeth.

Jessie pushed past Cora-Ann, took the tube, and began to read. "If eye or mouth contact occurs—"

She raised her eyes to Emily. Emily waved her hands wildly. "Come on! Come on!"

Then her lips stuck together. She let out a terrified growl. She couldn't speak at all.

"If eye or mouth contact occurs, rinse thoroughly but gently with water only," Jessie read. "Then get immediate medical attention."

For a moment no one moved.

Then Cora-Ann cried, "I'll call 911!" She ran out of the room.

She came running back a moment later. "They said we should drive you over to the emergency room. And don't worry. You'll be okay."

Mrs. Wallner came running in. Then came Rich. And Nancy. And Mr. Wallner. The whole family crowded into her bathroom, all talking at once.

"Well," Jessie said grimly, her arm around Emily's shoulders, "we know one thing. We know this was no accident."

Emily couldn't speak. So she pointed. She pointed an accusing finger at Nancy.

Nancy instantly burst into tears. She wrapped her hands around her chest as if shielding herself. "I didn't do it. Why does everyone always—"

She ran from the room.

For a moment no one spoke.

Mr. Wallner broke the silence. "This has to end here. I mean it. It stops here!" He balled his hands into fists. "We have to be a family!"

Emily spent the next hour at the emergency room. Shadyside Hospital is turning into my home away from home, she thought bitterly.

Emily felt embarrassed. What if they ask me how I glued my teeth together? What do I tell them?

Finally an intern swabbed Emily's teeth with a special chemical. He told her to be very careful not to swallow any of the clear liquid. Once he got her mouth open, he made her rinse and spit about a hundred times.

Emily could still taste something sharp and bitter in her mouth as her parents drove her home.

Jessie and Cora-Ann were sitting on the bottom of the front stairs when Emily came in the front door. They had waited for her. That was nice. So nice, in fact, that Emily immediately started crying again.

They all ended up hugging.

"Come on," Cora-Ann said finally, resting a hand on Emily's shoulder. "We'd better get to school. That is, if you feel up to it."

Emily felt a rush of warm feelings for Cora-Ann.

"Well, Cora-Ann," Jessie said as she pulled on her coat. "I think it's official now. You're a member of our wonderful family."

Cora-Ann rolled her eyes. "It's still better than *my* family," she said softly.

"Don't forget your bag," Emily told her as they started for the door.

The white canvas overnight bag stood next to the closet. "Oh, thanks," Cora-Ann said. "I guess somebody brought it down for me."

Butch ran in from the den to see them off. He flopped down, waiting to be petted. Emily knelt to tickle his tummy. Butch is so wonderful, Emily thought. Even on a day like today, he made her feel better.

Outside, they headed for Cora-Ann's car. "Come on, Cora-Ann," Emily said, "cheer me up. Tell me about what's going on at *your* house."

"Well," Cora-Ann began, "my mom is thinking of moving us all back to Parkerstown. That's for starters."

Jessie stopped short, halfway down the icy walkway. Emily and Cora-Ann both turned back to her.

"Move back *where?*" Jessie demanded.

Cora-Ann frowned. "Parkerstown?"

"Parkerstown *where?*"

"Ohio?"

Jessie stared hard at her. "Jolie was born in Parkerstown," she murmured.

For some reason Cora-Ann turned bright red. "She was? I mean, uh . . . Jolie? Is that the girl who died?"

Jessie narrowed her eyes at her. "How did you know that? I never told you about Jolie."

Cora-Ann was still blushing. "Huh? I guess someone else told me about her, then."

Emily stared at Cora-Ann.

Why is she blushing like that? Emily wondered. What is going on here?

chapter

18

Murder

*E*mily didn't get a chance to talk to Jessie until fifth period French, the only class they shared this semester.

Miss Clark was writing a long list labeled "Le Verbe Subjonctif" on the blackboard. She had her back turned.

Jessie leaned over and scribbled in Emily's notebook: "I'm very suspicious."

Emily raised her eyebrows as if to say, "Tell me more."

"Cora-Ann," Jessie wrote underneath her first note, then underlined it.

"Y?" wrote Emily, keeping her head down, as if she were copying what the teacher chalked on the board.

Jessie shrugged. "I just feel like she's up to something."

"Y?"

Jessie stopped writing. "I just do," she whispered. She glanced toward the front of the class. The teacher kept writing. "I mean, how did Cora-Ann know about Jolie?"

Emily shrugged. "That's no big deal," she whispered back. "You know how everyone here gossips about everyone. Every kid at Shadyside High probably knows about Jolie by now."

Jessie shook her head. "I just think it's weird. She's never mentioned Jolie to me before."

"Josette et Emilie," Miss Clark said sternly, her back still turned. *"Arretez de chuchoter!"*

Arretez de chuchoter! Miss Clark was always yelling that. Years from now, thought Emily, it will be the only thing I know how to say in French. "Stop whispering!"

Jessie started writing another note in her own notebook, then moved the notebook to the side of her desk so Emily could see. "How can we find out more about Cora-Ann? I'm like her only friend."

"Parkerstown," Emily wrote back.

Jessie shook her head. "I don't know anyone in Parkerstown," she wrote. "Do you?"

Emily shook her head no. "Forget it," she wrote. "A waste of time. Anyhow," she added, "what could we find out?"

Jessie lowered her head and scribbled another note. It was triple-underlined.

I just can't stop thinking about it. Why did Cora-Ann blush and act so weird when I mentioned Jolie?

* * *

Butch waited at the door when Emily returned home from school. He barked wildly, eager for his walk. When she took him outside, he wanted to play.

Emily watched the dog trot over the snow. Her thoughts turned to Jessie and Cora-Ann.

Cora-Ann had acted strangely, Emily had to admit. But she still felt Jessie was overreacting. She had no reason to be so suspicious of her best friend.

Join the club, Emily thought bitterly. Suspicion is my middle name.

Suspicion. Suspicion.

She felt suspicious of Nancy. She felt suspicious of Rich.

Shaking away her unpleasant thoughts, Emily whistled and Butch raced across the yard to her, brown ears flapping. She crouched down so the dog could lick her face.

"Thank you, Butch," she said. "I needed that."

She patted his head. He ran off again. As she stood up, she saw a flicker of movement in a second-floor window.

Nancy's room.

She put a hand over her eyes, blocking out the glare of the sun off the snow.

Emily could see Rich and Nancy, standing in front of the window. They were talking heatedly. Gesturing with their hands. Both talking at once.

Weird, Emily thought, staring up at them.

What are they talking about so excitedly? Rich and Nancy never have two words to say to each other.

Very, very weird.

* * *

"Police say they have apprehended the killer and he is an escaped inmate from the Barrington State Asylum. The body was found just—"

Emily snapped the car radio off. She was in no mood to listen to a story about a murder.

It was Saturday night. It was also Emily's first time driving since the accident.

Stay calm, she told herself.

But her breathing was coming shallow and fast.

Tonight she and Josh had gone to see the new Jim Carrey movie. Very dumb and silly, which was about all Emily could handle, considering everything that had been going on.

After the movie Josh wanted to drive her home. He said they could leave her car in the lot so she wouldn't have to drive home so late at night.

Emily refused. She remembered the old saying about learning how to ride a horse. When you fall off, get right back on, or you never will ride again.

She'd been fine for the first few minutes. Then the car skidded on a patch of ice.

And all the memories of the accident came flooding back.

She saw the tree trunk loom in front of the windshield. And as the car crashed into it—in her mind—as the windshield shattered once again—in her mind, all in her mind—other pictures swept into the car.

Into her mind.

The spilled perfume running down the dresser. The

special dress, her special dress, cut so neatly down the middle. Nancy's foot shooting out, sending Emily tumbling headfirst down the stairs.

Nancy. Nancy. Nancy.

Not all in her mind.

The Super Glue in the toothpaste. The pain of her locked teeth.

Not in her mind.

The threat. The dread. The fear of being in her own house. The fear of her own sister.

Not in her mind. All true. All happening.

She pulled the car up the driveway. Feeling shaky. Feeling the dread. She parked outside the garage. Cut the lights. Pushed open the door and hurried inside.

Not in my mind. All real. All real.

The warmth of the house helped to calm her.

"Hey—Butch?" Where was he? Where was her greeting?

She listened. Silence. So quiet she could hear the hum of the refrigerator.

"Butch?"

He must be sound asleep somewhere, she decided. "Butch?"

She listened for the jangle of dog tags, the click of his toenails on the linoleum.

"Hey—" Lights on in the den. Voices. From the TV. Someone staying up late, watching TV—and holding Butch on his or her lap?

Emily tossed her coat down and started toward the den.

She was halfway across the living room when she saw the sweater on the floor.

The brown sweater someone had tossed—no.

No. Not a sweater.

Butch.

Dead on the floor.

chapter
19

"What Did I Do?"

Emily opened her mouth. No sound came out. Then she dropped to the floor. She cradled the little furry body in her arms.

Balls of dust clung to the fringes of Butch's long brown fur. She cleaned them off. Rocked him, rocked him.

And then, from deep inside her, a cry rose up. It was like the first rumblings that signal an earthquake. The cry rose into a shout. Emily threw back her head and wailed.

The den door flew open. Jessie ran in. She stopped short when she saw Emily and the dog. "Oh, no! Oh, wow! Is he—?"

Emily rocked back and forth, back and forth. Then she set Butch down carefully. She scrambled to her feet.

"Wait—" Jessie cried. "Where are you—"

Emily didn't listen, didn't stop. She started toward the stairs. *"Nancy!"* she shrieked.

She felt ready to explode. This was the second dog that Nancy had murdered. The second dog.

"Nancy!!!!"

"Emily!" cried Jessie, pulling Emily back. "Wait. You can't blame Nancy. You have no proof! Maybe poor Butch just died. A heart attack or something."

Violently Emily pulled herself free. "A heart attack? He's only one year old!" she wailed.

She turned back up the stairs. "NANCY!"

"Emily, you'll wake the whole—"

Emily slapped Jessie's hands away. She charged up the steps, stumbled, but kept going, taking several of the stairs on all fours before she regained her balance.

She kicked the door to Nancy's room. It didn't open. Locked! She started pounding the door with her fists.

Doors flew open down the hall. Emily saw her parents tying their bathrobes as they hurried toward her. At the other end of the hall, Rich appeared in his boxer shorts and T-shirt.

Emily kicked Nancy's door again. "I know you're in there!" she shrieked through her tears. "Come out so I can kill you!"

The door swung open. Nancy stood in her nightgown, eyes wide in shock.

"I'm sorry," Nancy murmured, blinking away sleep. "What's wrong?"

Emily hesitated. Her sister seemed so innocent, so

totally unaware. Despite her rage, Emily found herself wondering—did Nancy do it? *Was* she the one?

Then she lunged.

With a furious sob she grabbed Nancy by the throat.

She felt Jessie's arms go around her waist. Pulling her. Pulling her back, away from Nancy.

Mr. Wallner came thundering down the hall, bellowing for them to stop. "Emily—let go of her! Let go!"

"What did I do?" Nancy wailed. "What did I do?"

Jessie pulled Emily off Nancy.

"What did I do? What did I do?" Nancy cried it over and over, a shrill chant. Mrs. Wallner rushed to comfort Nancy.

"Butch is dead!" Emily shrieked at her mother. "Why are you comforting her? Butch is dead!"

"Another dog bites the dust," Emily heard Rich mutter.

So casual. So pleased. So happy that Emily's heart was broken.

With a cry of fury Emily spun around. She grabbed Rich by the shoulders and shook him. Shook him so hard his head bobbed.

"Did you do it, Rich? Did you? *Did* you? Have you gone *totally* psycho?"

Emily climbed into the car beside Jessie. Jessie turned the ignition and started to back out of the garage.

At the back of the yard Emily could see her step-father leaning over a shovel. He was digging a grave for Butch, struggling to push the shovel through the hard, frozen ground.

Emily stared out the window. A cold, gray Sunday afternoon. She felt as if they were driving through a thick, gray cloud. She wanted to disappear into a cloud.

Emily sighed. "Do you think I could stay at Cora-Ann's house tonight? I really don't want to be alone in the house with Nancy."

Jessie turned the corner, headed toward Cora-Ann's house. "Mom and Dad will only be away one night."

"I—I can't believe they'd leave us all alone—after what happened last night," Emily stammered.

"Emily, you know they have to visit your uncle Mark," Jessie scolded. "The poor man is in the hospital and—"

Emily pictured Butch, sprawled so lifeless on the living room floor. She uttered a sob.

"I can't live in the same house with Nancy," she told Jessie. "Mom is so worried about Nancy. But Nancy scares me. I admit it. I really think she's come back to *get* me."

Jessie kept her eyes straight ahead on the road. "Nancy says she didn't do it," she murmured.

"I can't believe Mom and Hugh are going away tonight," Emily repeated. "Not that Mom and Dad do anything to protect me when they're home," Emily added bitterly.

She stared out the windshield into the misty gray.

"I should tell Dad to dig me a grave, too," she said suddenly.

"Oh, Emily!" Jessie cried. "Stop!"

"I'm serious. You can't always be there to save me, Jess. Sooner or later Nancy is going to get me. It's only a matter of time."

"Don't talk like that."

Emily leaned her head against the window and closed her eyes.

"I was thinking," Jessie said. "After we pick up Cora-Ann, why don't we go down to the ASPCA—"

"Don't say it!" Emily cried, turning to Jessie.

Jessie shrugged.

"Don't even think it," Emily insisted.

"Okay, okay. I'm not saying anything," Jessie said, eyes on the road.

"Well, don't."

They rode in silence for several blocks. "Maybe today is too soon to get a new dog," Jessie said at last.

"Way too soon," Emily agreed. "Ten years from now is too soon!"

Sighing, Jessie pulled over to the side of the road. She parked. "Come on. Let's get Cora-Ann."

Emily sat for a moment, staring straight ahead. Jessie had to come around and open her car door.

They were about halfway up Cora-Ann's front yard when Jessie grabbed her arm.

"Stop!" Jessie whispered. She pulled Emily back behind a low hedge.

"Oh, no, I don't believe it!" Jessie moaned, staring at the house.

Emily followed her gaze.

Two people were stepping out of Cora-Ann's house. A middle-aged man and woman.

"Do you know them?" Emily demanded. "Who are they?"

"Jolie's parents!" Jessie whispered.

chapter
20

All in the Family

"It's Mr. and Mrs. Bowen!" Jessie gasped.

"Are you sure?" Emily whispered.

"Of course I'm sure. Come on." Jessie tugged at Emily's coat sleeve. "Hide! I can't face them. Please, I—"

Too late.

"Jessie?" the woman called from the porch, sounding very surprised. She started down the walk, taking careful steps around the patches of salted ice.

"Oh, no," Jessie murmured.

Well, they couldn't just stand there and pretend they didn't hear the woman, Emily decided. She pulled Jessie's hand, forcing her forward.

"Hi," Emily called, trying to sound cheerful.

They met Mrs. Bowen at the end of the walk. Jolie's father stopped a few feet behind his wife.

Mrs. Bowen stared hard at Jessie. She clasped her hands together in front of her.

"We didn't know you moved to Shadyside!" Mrs. Bowen exclaimed. "Goodness—what a shock!"

Jolie's father stepped forward, putting an arm around his wife's shoulder. "It's nice to see you, Jessie," he said. "It's been too long."

Emily could tell it was painful for the parents to see Jessie. That made sense. Seeing Jessie must remind them of their dead daughter.

"It's nice to see you, too," Jessie mumbled awkwardly.

"I'm Emily Casey," Emily chimed in, sticking out her hand. "Jessie's stepsister."

Mrs. Bowen shook her hand. Then they all stared at each other uncomfortably.

"It's because of me that Jessie moved to Shadyside," Emily said in a forced, jolly voice. "Well, because of my mom actually. Jessie's dad married my mom after my dad—"

She stopped. She was going to say "died." She didn't want to remind these poor people of death.

It was like that game where you tried not to think of a huge pink elephant. And so all you could think about was the elephant. Everyone was trying not to mention Jolie. It was as if her coffin floated right over their heads.

"We were just going out," Mr. Bowen said finally, breaking the uncomfortable silence, "or we'd invite you in."

Mrs. Bowen forced a smile. She turned to Jessie. "You must be here to see Jolie's cousin, right?"

Emily could feel Jessie tense up beside her.

"Jolie's *cousin?*" Jessie asked in a hollow voice. "You mean—"

"Why, yes," Mrs. Bowen said. "Cora-Ann."

chapter

21

Who Turned Out the Lights?

Mr. Bowen stepped forward abruptly and took one of Jessie's hands in both of his. "Good to see you, Jessie. Really. Come by and see us sometime." Then he turned to his wife. "Well, Harriet . . ."

"Yes, we really must . . ."

Emily stepped aside to let them pass. Jessie barely moved. The Bowens had to make their way around her.

Emily and Jessie watched them climb into their car.

"So *that's* it!" Jessie exclaimed as they drove away.

"Huh?" Emily replied. She felt dazed. What did it mean that Cora-Ann was Jolie's cousin? How could that be?

"Come on," Jessie said. She hurried back down the path.

"Where are we going?"

"To the car. And don't look back."

"Why not?" Emily asked, immediately turning back.

Jessie grabbed her arm. "Stop it. I think Cora-Ann might be watching us."

"So what?" Emily cried.

Jessie didn't reply. She pulled Emily to the car.

"Get in!" Jessie ordered. She gunned the motor. She started to drive off before Emily had closed her door.

"Wait a sec!" Emily cried.

But Jessie didn't wait. She peeled out, driving fast.

"Cora-Ann is Jolie's cousin," Jessie said finally, glancing over at Emily.

"I know that!" Emily said. "I was there, too, remember? I wonder why she never told us."

Jessie slapped the wheel with her hand. "I'm so stupid! I totally forgot that Jolie had a cousin."

"Why should you remember that? Everybody has cousins."

"A cousin who was totally freaked when Jolie died," Jessie added grimly. "A cousin who was so upset she didn't come to the funeral. And now she's wormed her way into my life."

"But why?" Emily asked, horrified. She felt as if she was about to come face to face with some awful truth.

"Revenge," Jessie said. "What else?"

"Revenge? How is Cora-Ann getting—"

"Don't you see?" Jessie cried. "All the bad things that happened—we thought they were against *you*. But they were against *me*."

"Excuse me?" Emily cried. "Jessie, don't you think

that's a little far-fetched? I'm sorry, but I was the one who drove into a tree. Okay?"

"Emily, I drove that car as much as you did. Cora-Ann could have messed up the brakes, hoping to kill me." Jessie thought for a moment. "Oh, no."

"What?"

"The night you had the accident? I told Cora-Ann I was going to drive over to see this guy. Corey Pitt. You know him. Anyway, Cora-Ann made me *promise* that I would go ahead with it. You know, surprise the guy. She triple-dared me. And then I couldn't drive over to see him because—"

"Because?" Emily asked in a tiny voice. She already knew the answer.

"Because you took the car to see Josh instead."

Emily stared at the road, watching the front of the car eat up the little sections of dotted white line. "No way," she said finally.

"Yes! It makes sense!" shouted Jessie. "Listen. The short black dress? The one I got the stain on? I was with Cora-Ann the night that happened. She probably thought it was *my* dress. Same thing with your fancy French perfume. I always wear that perfume. Cora-Ann knocked over the bottle, thinking she was hurting *me!*"

Jessie clutched the wheel so hard her knuckles turned white—

Emily shook her head, thinking hard. "I just don't buy it, Jessie," she said finally. "Why would Cora-Ann kill Butch? She knew Butch was my dog. Why would she kill my dog?"

"Who did Butch like best? You or me?" Jessie demanded.

"You hated Butch," Emily pointed out.

"That doesn't matter," Jessie replied. "All Cora-Ann ever saw was the dog jumping all over me. She probably figured I was the one who would be hurt the most by the dog's death."

They drove in silence. The sky, as if sensing their mood, had turned charcoal dark. It was as if night had fallen two hours early.

Emily's stomach turned. A wave of horror swept over her.

Jessie could be right, she realized.

Jessie could be right. Cora-Ann could be doing all these horrible things. Not Nancy. Not Nancy.

"Cora-Ann was there the morning the glue was in the toothpaste," said Emily thoughtfully. "She slept over and—"

They both stared at each other.

"She was trying to wake you up," Emily told Jessie, pounding the dashboard with her fist. "She wanted you to use the bathroom first!"

Emily felt the car pick up speed. They were taking the icy turns pretty quick. "Hey, slow down," Emily warned. "Or you'll kill us both."

Jessie didn't slow down.

Emily gasped as an explosion rocked through the car.

Thunder.

Jessie leaned forward, peering up at the sky through

the windshield. "Looks like that storm is going to hit us after all."

"What storm?"

"Where have you been?" Jessie asked. "You haven't heard? There's a big storm headed this way. The good news is it's not cold enough to snow today, but—"

Fat drops of rain pelted the windshield like a burst of enemy gunfire. A second later the rain started coming down in sheets, drumming on the roof of the car. Jessie set the windshield wipers on high, but even the rapid beating of the blades couldn't keep the water off the glass. The whole world had gone dark and blurry.

"I can't believe I accused Nancy," Emily uttered.

Jessie didn't say anything. She leaned forward, trying to see the road.

"Can you imagine how she must have felt? Every little thing that happened, I immediately started yelling, 'It's Nancy!' 'It's Nancy!' She probably wished she had stayed in the hospital."

Emily glanced over at Jessie, saw her concentrating on her driving.

"When we get home," Emily said, "I'm calling Mom and Dad at Uncle Mark's. Telling them to come right home."

"They won't be there yet," Jessie replied. She glanced at the dashboard clock. "They probably just left."

"Jessie," Emily said, "I know what you're going through. You're scared. You think Cora-Ann is after you. But don't worry. I'll protect you. Just as you've been protecting me. She's not going to hurt you."

Another explosion made Emily jump.

More thunder. Up ahead, jagged streaks of lightning ripped the gray sky, bright cracks in a wall of darkness.

Jessie drove up the driveway so fast she almost crashed into the closed garage door. They raced inside through the downpour, pulling up their hoods as they ran.

"Nancy?" Emily called as they came rushing in the front door.

No reply.

Jessie locked the front door behind them. Both locks.

Emily ran up the steps. "Nancy?"

Her bedroom door was locked.

"Nancy?" she said quietly. "Are you in there? Hey, can I come in?"

Silence. Then her sister called coldly, "What do you want?"

Emily leaned her head against the door. She could feel drops of cold water running down from her hair. "Nancy, I'm so sorry."

More silence.

"Why?"

"For accusing you, blaming you."

Silence.

"Nancy, I just found out. I know it wasn't you. I mean, with Butch. And everything else. It was Cora-

Ann. She's Jolie's cousin. She's been doing all this stuff to get back at Jessie."

"Right," Nancy called bitterly through the door. "That's what you say now. Wait till the next bad thing happens. Then who are you going to blame?"

"Nancy, please let me in." Emily rattled the door-knob. "We've got to talk."

No answer. Then: "Go away Emily. I'm working on my mural."

"I'll come back in a few minutes, okay, Nance?" Emily pleaded. "I've got to get out of these wet things."

Nancy didn't answer. Emily waited. Finally she rushed down the hall and into her room.

Don't worry, she told herself. Now that you know it wasn't Nancy, you can make it up to her. You'll get her to forgive you.

She peeled off her wet parka, shook water from her hair. Her big smock felt dry.

Jessie hurried into the room, unzipping her coat.

"I kept getting a busy signal," she said, tossing her keys on the bed.

"Where? What do you mean?"

"At your uncle Mark's. I was trying to reach Mom and Dad."

"Try again," Emily urged.

"Right." Jessie reached for the phone. But it started to ring before she could pick up the receiver. She drew back her hand.

"Well? Aren't you going to pick it up?" Emily cried.

Jessie lifted the receiver to her ear. Listened.

"Hi, Cora-Ann," she said, her voice breaking.

"Don't say a word," Emily whispered, waving her arms. "Don't tell her—"

"We know everything!" Jessie blurted out. "We know you're Jolie's cousin! We know what you've been doing! Don't call here, ever again!"

She slammed down the receiver.

The overhead light went out.

"Hey—what's going on?" Emily cried. She groped her way to the door and tried the switch.

No light.

Then she saw that the hallway light was out, also.

"Oh, no," she groaned.

"The storm," Jessie said softly in the darkness.

"No electricity," Emily groaned.

She squinted at the blurred outline of her stepsister in the darkened room. Outside, she could hear the wind whipping the trees, making the branches creak like bones about to snap.

Now what? Emily thought.

Now what?

chapter

22

Knock, Knock

"It's so dark," Emily said softly. "As dark as midnight."

Trailing their hands along the wall, they made their way down the front steps. "There have to be some candles somewhere," Emily said.

They tried the kitchen first, groping around blindly in the drawers.

"Ow!" Jessie gave a sharp cry.

"What is it? Are you okay?"

"I stabbed myself on something," Jessie moaned. She held the object up close to her face, staring at it. "Can opener." She tossed it back in the drawer.

"Where does Mom keep candles?" Emily asked herself.

"Or a flashlight."

"Maybe in the tool kit," Emily said.

But that was in the garage. She wasn't going to the garage. Not now.

She pictured the candles. She could see the yellow wax, the long thin box. Now what was next to the box?

A deck of cards?

"I remember. There are candles in the dining room in the sideboard," she told Jessie. "Next to the good decks of cards—you know, the ones Mom won't let us play with."

"Right!" Jessie agreed. She moved quickly to the dining room.

Emily could hear Jessie rustling around in the dining room, could hear the scrape of wood as she opened the sideboard drawer.

The wind roared. Emily felt cold air biting her skin. There was an open window in the living room, she realized. Rain pouring in.

Emily started toward the open window, her eyes slowly adjusted to the dim light.

"I found the candles," Jessie called. "Now all we need are—"

A loud knock at the front door interrupted her.

Emily gasped.

Who could it be?

"Emily? Was that you?" Jessie called, frightened.

Emily didn't answer. She moved to one side of the open window, peering out at the front porch.

Another knock, louder than the first.

"Who is it?" she heard Jessie call from the dining room.

Emily pressed her face against the wall, trying to see out the window to the porch.

She caught a glimpse of a blue parka.

Dark hair.

A bolt of jagged lightning lit up the porch.

It was like a flash picture, a picture that seared into Emily's brain.

Cora-Ann. Her dark hair plastered by rainwater to her skull. Knocking on the door.

Cora-Ann, holding that big knife of Rich's.

Waving it in her hand.

chapter
23

Knife Attack

B*ang bang bang bang.*

Emily shrank back. Was Cora-Ann pounding on the door with the heavy knife handle?

Bang bang bang. The insistent knocking rising over the rumble of thunder and the drumming of rainwater against the window.

Emily turned to see Jessie running to the front door. "Don't let her in!" Emily shrieked. "Don't let her in! She has a knife!"

Then she realized where Jessie was headed. To the hall phone on the side table. "I'm calling the police!" Jessie shouted.

But then Emily heard Jessie utter a weak groan. "Jessie—?"

"It's dead. The phone is dead."

Bang bang bang bang.

Did the storm knock out the phone? Or did Cora-Ann cut down the wires?

Emily shuddered. She peered out of the rain-smeared window. Craned her neck, trying to see the porch.

Gone.

Cora-Ann was gone.

Emily stared hard, listening to the steady roar of rain.

Yes. Maybe Cora-Ann really did leave. If only she would disappear. Give up. Vanish from their lives forever.

"She didn't go away," Jessie choked out. "She's looking for another way in."

Emily froze.

"She can't get in—*can* she?" Jessie demanded in a tight, shrill voice.

"I—I don't think so," Emily stammered. "Let's check the doors and windows!"

They both started across the kitchen to the back door.

Too late.

With a roar of rain-drenched wind, the kitchen door swung open.

Cora-Ann burst through, eyes wild. Breathing hard.

Rainwater puddled around her as she charged across the room.

Shaking off water, she shoved past Emily.

Raised the knife.

And moved in on Jessie.

chapter
24

Nancy to the Rescue

*E*mily uttered a scream of horror.

Jessie raised her hands as if to shield herself. "Cora-Ann—please!" she begged.

Cora-Ann hesitated, rainwater dripping down her face.

Emily turned and saw a figure step into the kitchen doorway.

Nancy!

Nancy moved quickly across the kitchen. She stepped up to the counter. Pulled a heavy iron frying pan off the wall.

Cora-Ann still hadn't seen her. She had her back to Nancy.

The big knife trembled in Cora-Ann's upraised hand.

She started to turn—as Nancy swung the heavy metal pan.

The pan made a dull *thock* as it hit the back of Cora-Ann's skull.

Emily heard a cracking sound.

Cora-Ann's mouth gaped open. Her eyes bulged. Confused. Then pained.

"Unh." A short grunt escaped Cora-Ann's throat.

The knife fell from her hand and bounced over the floor.

Her knees bent. She crumpled to the floor. "Unh." Another short grunt.

Then silence.

She didn't move.

Nancy stood over her, staring down, her shoulders hunched, the heavy pan in both hands.

"Nancy!" Jessie cried in a high, shrill voice.

Emily tried to talk, but uttered only a hoarse choking cry.

"Nancy!" Jessie repeated. "You saved us! Cora-Ann—she's crazy! Crazy! She's been doing all those things. The things we thought you did. Cora-Ann did them all. To get back at me. She must think I killed her cousin."

Nancy hadn't raised her head. She stared down numbly at Cora-Ann's motionless body. Emily saw Nancy's whole body convulse. Nancy made a loud gulping sound.

"Nancy—it's okay!" Emily whispered.

It's finally over, Emily thought, staring at her sister. Finally we can put the horror behind us. We can be a family again.

Nancy saved Jessie and me from Cora-Ann, Emily

told herself. Now maybe Nancy can forgive herself for what she tried to do to me a year ago.

Now we can all forgive each other.

And be a family.

"Nancy—thank you!" Jessie cried. She rushed toward Nancy with her arms outstretched.

Nancy raised the heavy pan with both hands. She pulled back—and swung with all her might.

The pan caught Jessie behind her right ear.

Jessie opened her mouth in a high-pitched whinny. Dark blood spurted from her ear.

Her eyes rolled up in her head. Her hands flew up into the air.

Then she collapsed beside Cora-Ann on the rain-spotted linoleum.

Emily gaped in shock. She didn't have time to scream or cry out or move.

Nancy quickly stepped over Jessie's fallen body.

She pulled back the frying pan again and narrowed her eyes at Emily. "You're next," she said softly.

chapter
25

Stabbed

"Nancy—n-no!" Emily stammered.

She started to back away, moving toward the kitchen door.

"Why did you hit Jessie?" Emily demanded, staring through the darkness at her sister's twisted scowl. "What are you *doing?*"

Nancy didn't reply. To Emily's surprise, she lowered the frying pan. Then she tossed it to the floor. It clanged loudly, bounced twice, came to a rest beside Jessie's sprawled body.

"Nancy—please!" Emily begged. Her eyes moved to the doorway. Can I get out of this house before she catches me? Emily asked herself.

Probably not.

Jessie and I double-locked the front door, Emily remembered.

Nancy ducked down behind the counter, disappearing for a moment. When she stood up, she held the knife.

"Nancy—listen to me," Emily pleaded. "Put that down. We have to get help. We have to get help for Cora-Ann and Jessie. We can't just leave them lying here."

Nancy finally spoke. In a low voice, distant and strange. "Cora-Ann must have taken my bag by mistake," she told Emily.

"Your . . . bag?" Emily kept her eyes on the knife, raised in Nancy's hand.

"My white canvas bag," Nancy explained in the dull, low voice Emily had never heard before. "I left it downstairs by the steps. Cora-Ann must have thought it was her bag. She took it."

"I—I don't understand," Emily stammered.

From the floor, Jessie let out a low groan. She didn't move.

"Cora-Ann opened the bag and found my knife," Nancy continued, taking a menacing step toward Emily. "That's what must have happened. She found my knife and came running over here in the rain. She couldn't wait to show you what she found."

"*Your* knife?" Emily cried. "You mean it isn't that knife from Rich's video?"

Nancy waved the knife. "My knife. Mine. My most precious possession. She almost ruined it for me, Em. Cora-Ann almost ruined it for me."

"But, Nancy—" Emily pleaded, taking another step back.

139

"I've waited a whole year, Em," Nancy continued. "I waited to pay you back. A whole year. I kept my knife hidden in my bag, and I waited. I pretended to be cured. I fooled the doctors, Em. I fooled them all. I pretended to lose my anger. Pretended."

Nancy let out a long, bitter sigh. "I knew it was the only way to get back here. The only way to pay you back for ruining my life."

"And so you did all those things?" Emily demanded, stalling, stalling for time. "You tripped me on the stairs? You spilled the perfume? You messed up the brakes and murdered my dog?"

Nancy nodded. "Yes. I waited a whole year. A whole year—for this." She raised the knife. Lurched forward.

"No!" Emily screamed. "Nancy—no!"

But her pleas were ignored.

Nancy plunged the knife down into Emily's body.

chapter

26

Hate Hate Hate

The knife tore through the fabric of Emily's huge smock.

The blade tangled in the folds of cloth—and missed Emily's body.

Missed her. Missed her.

Emily let out a long *whoosh* of air as she felt the smock rip. She saw Nancy's face twist in surprise, in fury. Nancy struggled to free the knife from the bulky smock.

But Emily grabbed her arm. Swung her away.

And started to run.

Running blindly through the darkened house. Down the front hall. Then up the stairs.

Running. Running *where?*

Into the first open doorway.

Too frightened to stop. Too frightened to think. Her heart pounding. Such a close call. So close.

But she knew she was still not safe.

141

"Emily?" Nancy's voice from the stairs, calm and low again.

Emily shivered, struggling to catch her breath.

"Emily—don't run from me," Nancy called. Closer. "I've waited a whole year, Em. Don't spoil it for me."

Where can I hide? Emily asked herself, feeling her throat tighten in panic. I'm trapped here. Where can I hide?

Behind the door. Her entire body trembling now.

"Emily—don't hide from me." Nancy so close. Inches away. In the doorway. On the other side of the door.

Close enough to hear Emily's rasping breaths.

And the lights flickered on. So bright.

Emily blinked.

And Nancy stepped into the room. Stepped up to her. "Here you are, Em!" The knife blade gleamed in the light.

"Noooooooo!" Emily let out a wail of protest. She lowered her shoulder—shoved Nancy aside.

Startled, Nancy stumbled back.

Emily heard a lamp crash to the floor. Heard Nancy's angry curse.

Emily plunged across the room. Everything a bright blur.

Too bright. Too bright. Somehow the darkness felt safer.

She stumbled into the wall. Her hands grabbed the sheet.

The sheet over Nancy's mural.

Emily pulled. The sheet fell away.

Nancy's mural came into view. Her painting. Her artwork.

Emily gaped at the wall. At the words. HATE HATE HATE. The word scrawled in red paint. Bloodred paint.

HATE HATE HATE HATE HATE HATE.

Scrawled on the wall. Smeared on in thick red paint.

Over and over.

One word. One message.

Nancy's mural.

Before Emily could turn away, Nancy charged.

But Emily wrapped her arms around her sister. Hugged her.

Hugged her.

Hugged her.

"You're my sister. You're my sister, Nancy. Don't hate me. Please don't hate me!"

Hugged Nancy. Hugged her. Tighter. So tight Nancy couldn't move. Couldn't raise her arm. Couldn't raise the knife.

Hugged her.

"Don't hate me! I'm your sister. I forgive you. I forgive you!"

It was true, Emily realized. For the first time, it was true. "I forgive you. I forgive you."

She hugged her. Hugged her.

Emily heard the front door slam. "We're back," her mother called. "The road was all washed out in Falls River."

She was still hugging Nancy as her parents burst in a few seconds later.

"What's going on here?" Mr. Wallner demanded. "What's *happening?*"

It would take a long time to explain.

"Cora-Ann says that her parents finally went to a marriage counselor," Jessie announced. "And after only one session, the counselor told them they should definitely get divorced. They're finally going to do it, too."

"That's great," Emily said, forking a pile of mashed potatoes onto her plate.

"Huh? That's great?" Mr. Wallner cried from the head of the table.

"Yeah," Jessie replied with a laugh. "I know it doesn't sound like good news. But it is. At least they won't be fighting in front of Cora-Ann all the time."

It was Sunday night. Three Sundays had gone by since *that* Sunday—the night of Nancy's attack.

I should feel so horrible, thought Emily.

Nancy was back in the hospital. Probably for a long stay.

But at least this time Emily was allowed to visit. And she'd been going every week.

Emily meant what she said when she hugged Nancy. She had finally forgiven her sister. It was like a huge weight off her shoulders. A weight she never even knew was there.

"So, Jessie, I guess that means you forgave Cora-

Ann, huh?" Mrs. Wallner asked, pouring another cup of tea.

"Mom, get with the program," Jessie replied. "That was last week!"

Emily recalled the whole story. How Cora-Ann had admitted that she was spying on Jessie, trying to find out if Jessie had really killed her cousin. But that was only at first.

After a few weeks Cora-Ann just wanted to be Jessie's friend. Cora-Ann really needed a friend.

Mr. Wallner stared off toward the den. "Rich! Your food's getting cold. Where is that boy?"

"Watching TV," Jessie told him.

"I'm going to count to ten!" Mr. Wallner called.

A door opened. "One more minute," Rich pleaded back. "This show is almost over."

Mr. Wallner rubbed his face with both hands. "What's so important? What's he watching?" he asked.

Emily giggled. *Family Feud!"*

About the Author

"Where do you get your ideas?"

That's the question that R. L. Stine is asked most often. "I don't know where my ideas come from," he says. "But I do know that I have a lot more scary stories in my mind that I can't wait to write."

So far, he has written over fifty mysteries and thrillers for young people, all of them bestsellers.

Bob grew up in Columbus, Ohio. Today he lives in an apartment near Central Park in New York City with his wife, Jane, and fourteen-year-old son, Matt.

THE NIGHTMARES
NEVER END . . .
WHEN YOU VISIT

Next . . .
SUPER CHILLER #9:
The New Year's Party
(Coming mid-November 1995)

Reenie Baker and her friends love to scare each other by playing dead. They compete to come up with the most realistic fake blood, the best fall, the best scream.

Then at Reenie's Christmas party, one of the tricks goes wrong. Very wrong. P.J. Fleischer ends up dead.

Two of the kids who were in on the joke are murdered. And Reenie's afraid she could be next. Especially when she arrives at a New Year's Eve party—and finds the entire room decorated in black.

Will Reenie be alive to celebrate the new year?

FEAR STREET®

R.L. Stine

- ☑ THE NEW GIRL.................74649-9/$3.99
- ☐ THE SURPRISE PARTY....73561-6/$3.99
- ☐ THE OVERNIGHT.............74650-2/$3.99
- ☐ MISSING.........................69410-3/$3.99
- ☐ THE WRONG NUMBER......69411-1/$3.99
- ☐ THE SLEEPWALKER.........74652-9/$3.99
- ☐ HAUNTED.......................74651-0/$3.99
- ☐ HALLOWEEN PARTY........70243-2/$3.99
- ☑ THE STEPSISTER.............70244-0/$3.99
- ☑ SKI WEEKEND..................72480-0/$3.99
- ☑ THE FIRE GAME...............72481-9/$3.99
- ☑ THE THRILL CLUB.............78581-8/$3.99
- ☐ LIGHTS OUT.....................72482-7/$3.99
- ☑ TRUTH or DARE................86836-5/$3.99

- ☐ THE SECRET BEDROOM......72483-5/$3.99
- ☐ THE KNIFE........................72484-3/$3.99
- ☑ THE PROM QUEEN..............72485-1/$3.99
- ☐ FIRST DATE......................73865-8/$3.99
- ☐ THE BEST FRIEND..............73866-6/$3.99
- ☐ THE CHEATER...................73867-4/$3.99
- ☐ SUNBURN.........................73868-2/$3.99
- ☐ THE NEW BOY...................73869-0/$3.99
- ☐ THE DARE........................73870-4/$3.99
- ☐ BAD DREAMS....................78569-9/$3.99
- ☐ DOUBLE DATE...................78570-2/$3.99
- ☐ ONE EVIL SUMMER.............78596-6/$3.99
- ☐ THE MIND READER..............78600-8/$3.99
- ☐ WRONG NUMBER 2.............78607-5/$3.99
- ☐ DEAD END ....86837-3/$3.99
- ☐ FINAL GRADE....................86838-1/$3.99
- ☐ SWITCHED.......................86839-X/$3.99
- ☐ COLLEGE WEEKEND...86840-3/$3.99
- ☑ THE STEPSISTER 2........89426-9/$3.99

SUPER CHILLER

- ☐ PARTY SUMMER...............72920-9/$3.99
- ☑ BROKEN HEARTS..............78609-1/$3.99
- ☑ THE DEAD LIFEGUARD....86834-9/$3.99
- ☐ BAD MOONLIGHT..............89424-2/$3.99

CATALUNA CHRONICLES

- ☐ THE EVIL MOON..........89433-1/$3.99
- ☐ THE DARK SECRET.....89434-X/$3.99
- ☐ THE DEADLY FIRE ......89435-8/$3.99

Simon & Schuster Mail Order
200 Old Tappan Rd., Old Tappan, N.J. 07675
Please send me the books I have checked above. I am enclosing $_____ (please add $0.75 to cover the postage and handling for each order. Please add appropriate sales tax. Send check or money order—no cash or C.O.D.'s please. Allow up to six weeks for delivery. For purchase over $10.00 you may use VISA: card number, expiration date and customer signature must be included.

Name _____

Address _____

City _____ State/Zip _____

VISA Card # _____ Exp.Date _____

Signature _____

739-24

Tombstones™

DANCES WITH WEREWOLVES

Holly Brand is a heroine! She stopped a mad killer in the act. Only Holly, her friend Zakiya, and police chief Dorn know the truth — the killer was a werewolf. But it's not over. The werewolves are here and they're coming to the dance. This time she'll have to save the last one for them...

John Peel

☐ Dances with Werewolves 53529-3/$3.99

An Archway Paperback

Published by Pocket Books